KISS & MAKEUP

BEAUTY SECRETS MYSTERY 2

STEPHANIE DAMORE

PINK SAPPHIRE PRESS

To Jimmy Johns,
For feeding my kids so I could write.
Thank you.

"*B*ut is it too white?" Aria stared at herself in the floor-length mirror.

I glanced up from my phone, totally over this whole wedding-dress business. What was supposed to be a thirty-minute dress fitting had turned into a three-hour ordeal. Never mind the fact that it was also my birthday and Aria had completely forgotten it. Add that to the fact that she had tried on dozens of gowns before settling on this one two months ago; and now at her final fitting, she was having second thoughts? You could see my annoyance.

The seamstress, Aria's cousin, and the other bridesmaid —Christina—were all doing their best to reassure her. "Too white? Impossible. You look gorgeous," Christina said. She walked around Aria, fluffing and primping the dress. Christina was a perfectionist and she liked everything just so, including her nude-colored manicure and her intricate hair braids. I tried to ignore her, which was my general MO when it came to Christina. She always thought she was right. Always has.

"Simply beautiful," the seamstress said.

I sided with Aria. One: she hated wearing white. In fact, Aria gravitated toward brighter colors. Red was more her style. And two: the fit was all wrong. Don't get me wrong, the high-necked beaded lace gown was gorgeous, but it just wasn't Aria. I would've told her all this the first time around but, well, I wasn't there. I had been so busy expanding my beauty business that I hadn't had much time to help Aria plan her wedding. No matter. It seemed Christina was stepping up and filling that role, even if she was only a bridesmaid again. A fact that I think she mentioned just twice today. An improvement.

"Girl, what do you think?" Aria looked over at me for approval.

Crud. She knew I couldn't lie to her, but her wedding was only a week away. As in, she had exactly six days until she'd become Mrs. Vincent Delgado. She didn't have much time to order a new custom gown.

"Sorry." I put down my phone. "I was just texting Mrs. DeVine. I told her about that rental space. Remember the one I told you about on Main? I think it's perfect, and she agrees. Gotta talk a few more business details with her later in the week."

Mrs. DeVine was the investment backer for my new beauty business. I had managed to fund the initial research and product run, but that was about as far as my ex's engagement ring had gotten me. Without Mrs. DeVine's support, my business would've been operated out of my apartment for the foreseeable future. I was incredibly lucky to have her on board, but that also meant needing to run things by her and stay in her good graces, which also meant attending the social events she hosted once a month. These gatherings were basically a giant cocktail party for the rich and famous of Savannah, with a little business networking thrown in. The next one was this upcoming Wednesday and I promised her I'd be there, even if I'd rather be at home binge watching Netflix.

"Is that a hive?" I took a closer look at my bestie's face. Her usual warm skin tone was turning into a blotchy mess. "Girl, you gotta calm down. You know you could wear a trash bag and Vince would still marry you." True story. The man adored her. Plus, he was filthy rich, which somehow made it even more exciting. He bought islands and fancy cars the way some people bought shoes or scratch-off lottery tickets. (Hey, don't judge.)

"You're right." Aria took a deep breath.

I stood up from the cream-colored couch. "Listen, I'd love to continue our little party, but I have a hot date and a cake with my name on it waiting for me."

It was Seaside Days. The annual kick-off-the-summer festival Port Haven was known for. Finn was going to meet me there to celebrate my birthday and watch the bake-off action. Mrs. Birdie Jackson, aka Mrs. J., the town gossip queen and my surrogate nana, was after the championship title and the competition was fierce. I wouldn't miss it for the world, even if she didn't also have a birthday cake waiting for me. Not to mention the fact there were plenty of free samples to go around too. If I was lucky, maybe even a corn dog. Carnival eats should be their own food group.

"But, we're not done yet," Christina insisted, referencing the list on her ever-present clipboard.

"Oh, but you know me and cake," I said with a devilish smile.

"Oh, girl, I'm so sorry." Aria turned awkwardly to step down from the carpeted pedestal. The fabric twisted around her feet. I went to her instead. "I can't believe I totally forgot. Happy birthday!"

"It's okay, girl. You're a bit of a hot mess right now, but I still love you. I do have to go, though. Mrs. J. made my favorite." No need to elaborate. Everyone knew my favorite was Mrs. J.'s famous chocolate cake with its ooey-gooey filling and warm chocolate sauce on top. My mouth tingled in anticipation of the sugar. I may have even drooled.

"Mind if I come with?" Christina asked.

"Wha-? Uh, I guess not." What happened to not being done yet? I guess cake had the same effect on Christina.

"She's baking the wedding cake, right?" Christina asked. That she was. Aria had wanted to go with some vegan confection, but I talked her out of that nonsense. "Well, as Aria's unofficial wedding planner, I think I should taste it, to make sure it's good enough for our bride-to-be." Christina said the last part all sing song-y. *Oh brother.*

Aria shrugged her bare shoulders. "Just give me five minutes. I want to talk to the seamstress about our dresses and then I'll be ready."

Our dresses were a cranberry-satin number. Completely ugly, also Christina's doing.

"Okay, five minutes," I said. Maybe four and a half and then I was out of there.

MY MOM CALLED for the third time that day on the drive downtown.

"Ziva dear, you didn't answer me. Is Finn coming tomorrow?" Ugh, why wouldn't she just drop it? No way was I inviting Finn over to dinner at my parents. Birthday dinner implied a certain level of relationship status that I was trying to avoid. I had already learned that lesson and kept Finn a safe distance from my heart.

"Sorry, Mom. Not happening. He's taking off tomorrow for work. But I'll pass the invite on." *Liar, liar pants on fire.* But what was I going to say? My mother expected nothing less. She put the P in proper, which wasn't a surprise seeing that her mom and Mrs. J. had been best friends. Those ladies had spent a lifetime gathering dirt on everyone. The secrets those two must've known... My mom made sure none of them were about her.

I dropped the thought as we caught up to traffic. Seaside Days was the festival of the year for Port Haven. This event turned our small seaside town into a happening hot spot. The high school parking lot transformed into a carnival, Main Street was packed with sidewalk sales and street vendors, and the ocean-front park pavilion morphed into ground zero. This weekend's events featured an airshow, farmers market, country-music concert, and of course, fireworks. If you were a small-business owner, you cherished Seaside Days more than Christmas. I was planning on using the extra publicity to launch my own personal business— Serenity Now. I was introducing the spa line first as to not compete with my Beauty Secrets clientele. Privately, I already had friends raving about and reviewing my product line, but this weekend was going to be my grand public debut before opening my storefront next month (hopefully!). Thanks to the added investment of Mrs. DeVine, my business was blooming faster than I could have ever imagined. I needed everything to be perfect this weekend.

Parking, of course, was a nightmare, which is why I agreed to meet Finn at the marina where he worked, and we'd walk down together. I parked my cute little pickup next to his real truck on the scorched grass next to Murphy's Bait and Tackle. The spot had become my unofficial parking space.

Finn made his way down the docks as we turned the corner to search for him. His shirtless state and khaki cargo shorts put a smile on my face. *Happy birthday to me.* Before I met him, I had dubbed him the "shirtless hottie," and the nickname still fit.

Christina smiled at him a little too sweetly. I didn't blame her. He was smokin'.

"Happy birthday, babe," Finn greeted me with a kiss on the cheek. He lingered for just a moment, but it was long enough for me to take in the rugged, sexual scent of motor oil mixed with cologne that was quintessentially him.

"Do you girls want to come up?" Finn's studio apartment was above the bait shop. Thankfully, he had a separate outside entrance. The waterfront views were amazing. The sunrise? Not so much.

"No, that's okay. You run up. We'll wait right here." If Christina hadn't been with us, my answer would have been much, much different. I tempered down my thoughts by reminding myself that the bake off was set to start in forty minutes, and I didn't want to be late. I was sure it was going to be a mouthwatering event. Grand prize was also five thousand dollars, but it wasn't about the cash for Mrs. J. She was all about the bragging rights. If you asked me, she didn't need a title; she was the best baker in Georgia.

FINN WAS BACK DOWN at the docks and ready to go in less than ten minutes. Seriously, how did guys do that? I hadn't introduced Christina yet, so we took a few seconds to get that formality out of the way and then discussed our game plan. As far as Christina was concerned, she was only there to taste the cake and then be on her way. Knowing

Christina, she probably had a checklist that she *had* to get back to. That was fine by me. The girl was way more organized than I could've ever hoped to be. Even as kids, she had a love of making lists and she always insisted on being the teacher when we played school. Somehow, I always got detention.

We heard Mrs. J. before we saw her.

"Now you wait just a second, Paulette. I told the committee I was making this cake, and that's exactly what I'm going to do."

Paulette scrutinized the recipe card in her hand. Her salt-and-pepper hair swept across her face. She wore a silver headband that wasn't doing its job, but it did match the silver sequined blazer she wore. I had no idea how she could stand it. Not the sequins, although that was questionable, but the long sleeves with this heat. It had to be ninety degrees out.

"Well, I'm not even sure this recipe qualifies. It might be one of them copycat ones. You see them on the internet all the time," she said with authority in her voice. "And secret ingredients? Tsk-tsk."

"Copycat my foot! This here is my world-famous chocolate cake, and you know it. I'm not telling you what's in it either!" Mrs. J. had on a bedazzled apron, hot-pink-and-orange leggings, and a lime green shirt. She looked like rainbow sherbet. Crazy, yet somehow still coordinated. "Now, y'all better give me back my recipe and get out of my way. I've got some baking to do."

Paulette didn't move. She stared down Mrs. J. The last time this happened, someone got a pie to the face.

"Just think, next year I'll be a judge and you'll be baking for me!" Mrs. J. said. "Honorary Judge, there's nothing honorary here," she added under her breath. Last year,

Paulette won the competition and had been promoted to judge along with her best friend, Suzanne Butterfield, who I saw joining them now. Mrs. J. was still not over it. I didn't think she'd ever be.

"Ha! Over my dead body. You'll NEVER be a judge," Paulette said, puffing out her chest.

"Don't tempt me." Mrs. J. narrowed her eyes and took a fighting stance. My surrogate nana could deliver a threat like a boss. It was inspiring.

"Please, you hardly scare me." But Paulette took a step back. Suzanne looked behind her. I wondered if she was looking for a pie.

"Ladies, if you please." The town mayor, Mr. Humphrey Potts, hobbled over with his ivory-handled cane and tried to defuse the situation. "We have guests." His head motioned to the gathering crowd, in a nervous sort of way. The women ignored him. If he was smart, he would've just gotten out of the way. Mayor Potts wouldn't get anywhere with those two. This feud had been going on for years. They weren't about to stop. Besides, I never thought of Mayor Potts as an authority figure with his bumbling personality. The title Town Ambassador was more appropriate, which was probably why he was the festival's Grand Marshal every year.

"Admit it, that's why you're not baking this year. Couldn't handle a little competition," Mrs. J. said.

"Oh Birdie, you're pathetic. Must I remind you, *Deep South Cuisine* named my pecan torte Best of the Best," Paulette said.

"That's true, they did," Suzanne said, nodding her head to the gathering crowd.

"Well, whoopty flippin' do. I guess that settles it," Mrs. J. replied, twirling her finger in a circle.

"And you darn well know last year I won fair and square," Paulette insisted.

"If you call having relations with the festival's Grand Marshal fair and square..." Mrs. J. trailed off. Mr. Pott's complexion now matched his red bow tie. Suzanne covered her mouth with her hand and widened her eyes.

"Why you!" Paulette got all huffy. She turned her head to the right and then left in swift desperation, but no pies were in sight.

Mrs. J. smirked. I wasn't sure if I should laugh or be horrified. Finn found it totally amusing. Christina's eyes nearly bulged out of her head. I bet they didn't have drama like this at the country club.

"UGH!" Paulette turned on her heel and marched off, balling up Mrs. J.'s recipe card in her fist and throwing it on the ground. Suzanne threw an evil eye at Mrs. J. and followed Paulette. Mayor Potts trailed after them both, picking the card up and smiling at the crowd as if it had all been part of the show.

"Humph. I'd like to put a little something extra in her cake," Mrs. J. mumbled. I could relate. I had my own frenemy that brought out the worst in me. I tried to keep it in check, because, you know, Karma and all that; but man, sometimes ... Justine could irk me like no one else. *Speak of the devil,* I thought, as I saw her making her way through the crowd. She had her dolled-up poodle under one arm and was passing out flyers with the other. I didn't even want to know. I turned my back to her and got Mrs. J.'s attention.

"So, you ready to do this?" I asked her.

"Sug'!" Mrs. J. wrapped me in a giant hug. She smelled like chocolate and peppermint, and I drank it all in. She whispered, "And I see you brought Mr. Hot Pants, too." I gave her a little extra squeeze.

"Hey, this is Christina," I said when we broke free. "She's Aria's cousin. I told her you were making the wedding cake and she wanted to give it a little sample."

"Well, it's no buttercream; but if you ask me, this tastes better." Mrs. J. turned to the table behind her and came back with a bakery box filled with her chocolate cake. I opened the box and took in a big whiff. Forget a plate. Someone needed to get me a fork, stat!

"Happy birthday, sweets."

"Thanks, Mrs. J."

"You enjoy it, now. I got to be getting to work. The show starts in twenty minutes." Mrs. J. scooted us on our way.

We wished her luck and headed toward the makeshift food court, which was basically an open area with plastic tables and chairs, with food vendors outlining the perimeter. I didn't even let them sing "Happy Birthday" to me. We cut into the cake with a plastic knife and I doled out the deliciousness. Any skepticism Christina might have harvested vanished the moment that cake was in her mouth. I could see it in her eyes. Dessert nirvana. I'd be a total liar if I didn't say I would've eaten more than my fair share if Finn and Christina hadn't been there. The cake was that good. But, seeing that I was trying to be a lady (don't laugh) and we couldn't take a cake on the Ferris wheel, I thought it would be nice to give some away. So, I did. Satisfied with the cake, Christina took off, and Finn and I passed out the remaining slices on paper plates to whomever wanted one. Well, everyone except Justine. She tried to snag a piece from Finn (did I mention she was also his psychotic ex-girlfriend? Small world, huh?), but I told her no. And then I smiled.

Finn and I were back in the grandstands and ready to watch the show right when it started. Mrs. J. was cracking eggs, whisking batter, and adding a dash of this and that to her mixing bowls, all the while sporting a beaming smile as if she were on her own cooking show, laughing with the audience and telling stories about this or that. The other two contestants were all business. Wendy Swiss was making a caramel cake, and she looked like a total wreck. Even sitting three rows back, I could see her hands shaking. She was no competition. The other contestant, Mary Dubbs, was making miniature lemon soufflés. Although, I wasn't sure if she was making dessert or running a special op. She had everything from measuring spoons and candy thermometers to a citrus peeler and lemon zester strapped to the utility belt of her cargo pants. She even wore black army boots that looked like she was used to stomping out the competition. *Now, **she** might be a threat.*

Mrs. J. hummed as she worked until WA-WOOM! A small fire ball shot up from Wendy's stovetop. We all jumped back. I instinctively covered my eyebrows. It wouldn't have been the first time they were singed off. I liked to think I was a master at penciling in brows, but thankfully they were safe. We all stared as caramelized liquid bubbled and oozed over the pan and spilled across the cooktop. Wendy stood dumbfounded with a bottle of rum in her hand. Mrs. J. ran over and turned off the gas and pulled the pot from the flame. Military Mary didn't even look over. She was too busy zesting a lemon to death. Wendy burst into tears and ran off the stage, leaving Mrs. J. standing there with a literal hot mess on her hands. Mr. Humphrey arrived a moment later with a fire extinguisher and a roll of paper towels. With the chaos under control, Mrs. J. went back to her station and began whipping up her signature chocolate sauce. She was hilarious, trying to hide exactly what was in it, but I saw that she added a lot of butter and chocolate, and the last ingredient was some type of syrup. It looked like honey. I would've never thought to add that to a chocolate sauce. I'd have loved to ask Mrs. J. about it, but I knew she wouldn't elaborate. Regardless, I would've enjoyed licking that spoon.

When all was said and done, Mrs. J. had turned out a sensational cake. My mouth watered as I knew it tasted just as good. With two minutes to spare, she plated the judges' pieces, gave them one last drizzle of her special chocolate sauce, and turned them in. Military Mary had finished ten minutes earlier and was doing calisthenics on the sidelines. Wendy Swiss sat in the bleachers, still crying over her disastrous performance.

The judges sat at the front of the stage, analyzing the desserts from every angle, and deliberating in dramatic fashion while the audience waited with bated breath. A couple of middle-school band students were brought on stage to provide entertainment and ease the tension while we waited. Their rendition of *God Bless America* was about as good as you could imagine, and did little to settle the nerves that were dancing in my stomach. I wondered how Mrs. J. was holding up. I looked around to see for myself, but she was nowhere to be found.

Finally, after way too long and one too many musical versus, Mayor Potts was back front and center with a microphone in hand, ready to announce the winner. Mrs. J. popped back in place from wherever she had been, looking poised and ready to accept her award. I saw she was sporting fresh Passion Pout lipstick, a favorite hue of hers, and her apron had been tossed aside. Her confidence was contagious and I beamed at her in anticipation of her victory. I was just waiting to hear her name so I could rush over and congratulate her.

Finn put his hand on my bouncing knee. "Settle down,

cowboy," he said, and laughed. I swatted his hand away and shushed him. Mayor Potts was getting ready to speak.

"Should we get to it, then?" The mayor gave a bit of a nervous chuckle. "All right then! The winner of this year's Seaside Days championship bake off is ... drum roll please ... Mary Dubbs!"

Mic drop. The earth quaked in response, and I shivered.

Mary sprung onto stage like it had been a planned part of her workout. She pumped her fists in the air and bounced around the stage as if she had just knocked Mrs. J. out. The enthusiasm was all her own. A few people politely clapped, but anyone who knew Mrs. J. kept silent. I looked for Mrs. J. to see how she was handling the news, and did a double take. She was already rushing the stage. *Sweet sugar!* I leapt into action, but Mrs. J. was already having it out with Paulette before I could reach her.

"You rotten woman! That title is mine!" she shouted.

Paulette couldn't even get a word in.

"I hate you. This is just like you. You lie and you cheat, and I'm so sick of it!"

Mayor Potts stared at the ladies, who were having it out on the stage, horrified. I was pretty shocked too, and I knew how vocal Mrs. J. could be.

"You rigged this. So help me, Paulette. This doesn't end here!" Mrs. J. stormed off before turning and pointing at the mayor. "You too!" she threatened. Mayor Potts looked a little white around the collar. You did not want to be on Mrs. J.'s bad side, especially if you were in politics. If anyone could air someone's dirty laundry, it was Mrs. J. I didn't dare go after her. She needed to cool down about a thousand degrees before I'd touch her.

Mayor Potts gave another nervous laugh into the microphone. "Let's hear it once again for Mary! That was some dessert." He clapped. Mary clapped. The rest of the crowd was silent. *Awkward.*

I walked back off the stage and rejoined Finn. He looked at me with a huge grin. "Well, that was fun. Funnel cake?"

"You're terrible."

"What?" Finn looked all innocent. "C'mon, admit it. That was awesome. I bet someone posts it online." I really, really hoped they didn't, but Finn was probably right. I was sure it would go viral.

2

I should probably have felt like puking after all the junk I ate and carnival rides we rode. Funnel cakes, corn dogs, cotton candy, French fries, and that's only the stuff I remembered. Finn was a ride warrior. If it spun, swung, or dropped, he was all about it. I'd bet he'd go crazy at a real amusement park. Something to keep in mind. My head was still spinning.

The afternoon had finally ended and now it was time for my favorite part: fireworks. My birthday seemed to always be during Seaside Days. When I was little, I believed my dad when he said the fireworks were just for me. We had swung back by Finn's apartment for a blanket and a few drinks before heading down to the beach to claim our spot. The fireworks were launched off a barge straight in front of us. We couldn't have asked for a better view.

With the carnival behind us and the ocean in front, it was super romantic. My stomach churned again, only this time it had nothing to do with the carnival. *Maybe we should've made this a group thing.* Aria and Vince would've probably joined us. I could've still given her a call. I was a second away from texting Aria and seeing what she was up to, when Finn brought me back to the present. "Here. Happy birthday." He took a jewelry box out of his cargo shorts pocket.

Oh heck no. There better not be anything of the diamond variety in that little box. We hadn't been dating for that long. My heart pounded and I thought I'd pass out right then and there.

I must've looked terrified because Finn said, "Chill out, it's nothing like that. I know you."

I gave the phoniest laugh ever. Good grief, I was pathetic. I fumbled with the box and opened it. Inside was a beautiful silver charm bracelet with three charms: a high heel, a lipstick, and a champagne flute. He did know me, and well. "Finn, seriously, this is awesome. I love it." I kissed him full on the mouth in a beautiful public display of affection.

Finn rummaged in our little cooler and brought out a mini bottle of champagne. "I forgot the cups."

"That's okay." I was never one to turn down a little bubbly, and I could sure use a drink after my little freak out back there.

He popped the cork and handed me the bottle.

"Cheers, birthday girl. I have a feeling this year's going to be great."

"Me too." This *was* going to be the year. I had big dreams.

"So, tomorrow?" I asked.

"Yeah, sorry about that. Did you want me to see if someone else can take it?"

An offshore fishing trip had just been booked and Finn was set to take them out through the week. He had recently taken over the charter business for Mr. Murphy, and his trips had quickly built a following, thanks to his mad social media skills and his Instagram followers.

"No, it's cool. Seriously. Besides, you hate weddings as much as I do." With Finn out of town, there was no pressure for him to be my date. Bonus.

"I didn't say that. What I said was I didn't like them. You however, have serious wedding issues." *So very true.* This, of course, might have something to do with the fact that my ex-fiancé cheated on me two weeks before our wedding. Not going to lie, I still wasn't over it. Finn only knew part of the story, which was the way I planned on keeping it.

"Anyway, don't worry about the wedding. Not only that, but I have a bunch of work stuff going on. I'm sure the week will fly by."

"Just a girl boss."

"Building her empire," I said with a smile.

With a champagne bottle in hand and a gorgeous bracelet on my wrist, I leaned back, oohing and ahhing as the fireworks lit up the night sky. Did I know how to celebrate my birthday, or what? My favorite fireworks were the gold sparkly ones that popped and fizzed like giant Rice Krispies. Finn was all about the weeping willow ones that cascaded down the sky until dipping into the ocean. He pointed them out every single time, as if I could miss seeing them. I laughed at his innocence. The speakers on the grandstand played a mixture of eighties tunes and Americana music in sync with the blasts. It was a display of patriotism at its finest. With every explosion, the sand shook a little bit and the sensation reverberated in my chest. I loved it.

∾

THIRTY MINUTES LATER, the show was wrapping up. Blast after blast shot off from the barge in front. It almost looked like the platform was on fire with how quickly the shells were being launched. When the celebration ended, the entire beach and grandstands area erupted in cheers. I could already hear people saying how great the show was, comparing it to previous years. So far, everyone thought the town had done a fabulous job. We waited a few minutes while everyone seemed to make a mad dash, gathering their kids and gear, to beat traffic. Thankfully, we wouldn't be dealing with that mess.

"You about ready to head back?" I asked a few minutes later. I had only brought one of Finn's sweatshirts to throw over my cutoffs, and the night air had cooled several degrees.

"Yeah, let's go. I may or may not have a surprise waiting for you." Finn reached for my hand and brought it up to his lips for a kiss. Surprises weren't really my thing, but I had a feeling I'd love whatever Finn had in store.

"Beach or boardwalk?" he asked.

"Beach. Less crowded." Most of the crowd had thinned out except for the few bonfires that had popped up, and the kids who ran around on the beach with sparklers in hand.

I started to ask Finn more about his planned charter. "So, where are you going exactly?"

"Making a run from Savannah to St. Augustine with a couple of island stops along the way. It's basically the best vacation ever."

Ha, I doubted that. In my opinion, the best vacation involved the beach, a fruity cocktail, and my bikini. I turned my head and started to tell him so when I tripped over something and went flying face-first in the sand. My hands cushioned the blow, but I still took in a mouthful of grit.

"Hey, you okay?" Finn had dropped the cooler and blanket and rushed to my side.

"What the heck?" I rolled over and Finn gave me a hand up. I whipped the sand off my clothes and face, and tried to spit out the remnants in my mouth as ladylike as possible; but there was no proper way to do this, I discovered. At least I didn't get any in my eyes.

I looked behind me in the darkness to try and see what I had tripped over. "Sweet sugar!" I jumped back. A human foot was sticking out of the sand. Finn froze next to me and I knew he saw it too.

"Tell me this wasn't my birthday surprise," I said.

"Not even close."

I wish I could say this was the first dead body we'd found together. This time, I let him call the cops.

$\mathcal{T}$hanks to the added crowd control, two police officers arrived on the scene in less than five minutes. I pointed to where the body was and gladly stepped aside to let them do their thing. So far, only one foot was visible. I wasn't about to dig up any more.

Finn, on the other hand, didn't mind getting a closer look. "I think it's a woman." He had bent down to check it out. "Definitely. See? Her toenails are painted."

If anything could've gotten me to check out a dead foot, it would have been nail polish. I wondered if it was a Beauty Secrets color, but even that wasn't tempting enough. "I don't care. I'm not getting any closer." I crossed my arms and turned away, partly in defiance, but mostly because I was officially chilled to my core, and not because of the weather.

I spotted the detective before she even introduced herself. Two words came to mind when I saw her: blond bombshell. Her red lipstick matched the tank top that peeked out from underneath her brown bomber jacket. Her jeans were tight. Her blond hair was long. She looked absolutely nothing like my friend Detective Brandle. Where he was middle-aged and overworked, she was young and ambitious.

The uniformed officers motioned us and I prepared to answer twenty questions. The detective didn't say anything for minute, instead just looked us up-and-down with her intense, dark eyes. I know I was at a murder scene and all, but I didn't appreciate being scrutinized. After all, we're the ones who called the cops.

"Ziva Diaz," I said, extending my hand, growing more impatient by the minute. "This is my friend, Finn Hudson." I tried to ignore the look Finn gave me at the "friend" title. Who needed titles anyway? Titles just led to trouble.

"Detective Roxy," the woman replied with a firm handshake to both of us.

So, Foxy Roxy it was. She was beautiful for sure, but personally I thought she could do without the black eyeliner, given the dark red color she wore on her lips. It was a general beauty rule that you only played up one asset at a time. Dark eyes meant soft lips, and vice versa. You didn't want your makeup elements competing on your face, and you never wanted your look to cover up your personality.

"Ziva, come with me. Finn, I'll be with you in a moment," the detective ordered.

Smart move, separating the two of us before taking our statements, I thought.

"Okay, from the top," she said, once we were alone.

I kept it brief. The story really wasn't all that exciting. She only interrupted me once to ask, "Why did you disturb the body again?"

"I didn't do it on purpose. Didn't you hear the part about me tripping? In the dark?" *Hello?* I highly doubted running into a foot counted as disturbing a body, anyway. I might have to retract my "smart" comment. Either that, or she was trying to trip me up in my story. I wasn't ready to give her credit for that yet.

The sand was still gritty in my mouth, but I didn't want to spit it out in front of Detective Roxy. My mother did teach me some manners. Fortunately, she didn't object when Finn walked over and handed me a bottle of water.

"Thanks," I said to Finn as I took a drink. "I think that's about it," I said to Detective Roxy when I finished drinking.

The detective stared us down again. I put my hands on my hips and returned the stare. I had nothing to hide and the sooner she realized that, the sooner Finn and I could leave.

"Give me a few minutes with your friend here, and then you two can go," she said after a beat.

"Sounds good to me." I stepped aside and let Finn have his turn. I may have rolled my eyes as soon as I turned away from her. Did I mention I have issues with authority?

While they chatted, I tried to look anywhere but at the medical examiner. The methodical nature of their grim work creeped me out as much as finding a dead body. I could never be that calm while documenting death. The police had set up a barricade to keep the crowd away, and portable fluorescent lighting had been brought onto the beach, illuminating the scene like a baseball field. A man wearing a tan trench coat and matching fedora tried to peer this way and that, over the barricade and around the police. He had a cell phone in hand, and I think he was recording the scene, judging by the way he scanned the crowd with his phone raised up. My first thought was that he was a reporter, but then again, given his ridiculous get up, he might've been a Dick Tracy fanatic.

Mayor Potts arrived on the scene shortly thereafter. He paced back and forth from officer to officer, wringing his hands, and nodding his head a lot, mostly to himself. When that didn't seem to get him anywhere, he walked over to the crowd and did his best to reassure everyone that everything was all right. I even heard him say that it was just an "unfortunate accident." If he could explain how someone could accidentally be murdered and buried in the sand, I'd love to hear it.

"Ziva! Ziva! Pssst!" Someone hissed my name. I turned around, and I shouldn't have been surprised to see Mrs. J. standing at the barricade, trying to get my attention. She motioned for me to come over, but I wasn't sure if I should. I looked over to Finn, who was still deep in conversation with Detective Roxy. I glanced at the medical examiner and shuddered.

"Zee-va!" Mrs. J. used her mom voice. I shrugged my shoulders and ran over to her. She was pleased as pudding when I reached her. "Give me the scoop, honey girl."

"Mrs. J., how do you always know where to find trouble?" I was only half joking.

"Hush now. Who they digging up over there?"

"No clue. I just tripped over the body."

"Again? You gotta quit doing that, sug'." She had a point. Although, it had been a few months since I'd found my last dead body.

I looked back and saw Detective Roxy staring me down yet again. "Gotta go," I said to Mrs. J. and ran back to meet them. I gave Detective Roxy a look that said, *What, you didn't say I couldn't move.* I asked Finn if he was ready to go.

"Are we good here?" he asked the detective. She waved us away and started typing something into her phone.

Finn jogged back closer to the body to see if we could grab the stuff we had dropped. I left that task to him and thought of a question to ask Detective Roxy.

"Quick question for ya... Where's Detective Brandle?" I was hoping he had finally taken a vacation, but I doubted that was the answer.

"Surgery, ulcer. He'll be back in a few weeks." She didn't even look up from her phone.

"Ah, good to know." *I should send him a care package. But skip the sweets, his wife would kill me.* Detective Brandle was never very good at managing his sugar, and it probably wasn't good for an ulcer either.

Something caught my eye and I looked over before I could catch myself. It was the light reflecting off Paulette's sequined blazer. *Oh, that's not good*, I thought. She was the one who had been murdered and buried in the sand. I knew I wasn't the only one who saw it when the collective gasp moved through the crowd. I looked back behind me and saw Mrs. J. backtracking through the crowd as fast as her white sneakers would take her.

t's a little-known fact that I eat a lot of junk. Wait, who am I kidding? Everyone knows that the only vegetables I eat are the pickled ones in my bloody Mary. Sugar is my main food group. That, and maybe water. You know, to balance things out and eliminate all those free radicals. As a result, I forced myself to work out four times a week, which usually ended up being three times a week. No need to be an overachiever. Today was a cardio day, which meant running. Ugh, I hated running.

Finn's side of the bed had long been vacated and I could see the sunlight blasting in through the living room's front bay window. Finn didn't care about curtains as he was up every morning before sunrise (occupational hazard) and his bedroom didn't have windows.

I lay in bed for ten more blissful minutes before getting up to start my day. I refused to store anything at Finn's. Not even a toothbrush. But I did keep an overnight bag in my truck for these occasions, which were becoming more frequent, whether I wanted to admit it or not.

I quickly retrieved my bag, freshened up, and threw on a

pair of running leggings and a tank top. The June heat was sweltering. I would be a sweaty mess in thirty seconds. I planned on rewarding myself with a chai latte and coffee cake from Sweet Thangs when I was done (see, what did I say about my eating habits?), but I didn't have to. Finn had already left a strawberry cheesecake muffin next the coffee pot for me. He was right: he did know me well. Even better, he didn't try to change me. Aria, bless the girl, would've left me a carrot muffin or banana bread with flaxseed in it or something nasty like that. I considered Aria's regular diet a form of torture.

While I ate the muffin, I thought back to yesterday. It had been a birthday to remember, for sure. Finn's charm bracelet glimmered off my wrist in the sun. I thought about taking it off. It wasn't like I had to wear it twenty-four, seven, but I didn't want to lose it either. I decided to keep it on until I got home and could put it in my jewelry box. I thought back to Paulette and her comment to Mrs. J. yesterday. "Over my dead body," she'd said, which is exactly what I had tripped over. *Super ironic, but in a horrible way. I* also thought about Detective Roxy. Foxy Roxy was a force. She seemed like a good cop, but a bad people-person. She would have to ditch the whole staring-you-down bit; that wouldn't go over well here in small-town USA. You wanted people to like you. After all, one catches more flies with honey. I was glad I wouldn't have to deal with her anymore. I only hoped Mrs. J. would play it cool when Detective Roxy came calling; and believe me, she would come calling as soon as she heard about their little cat fight yesterday. Make that a whole life-time of cat fights. Mrs. J. better check her mouth before opening it to Detective Roxy. That would only get her into trouble.

I ate the last cheesecake-filled bite and smiled in satisfaction. *Time to run.* I tried to stifle my groans. Thankfully, I had an agenda to stick to for the day. Tomorrow was the farmers market and my big business debut. I wanted to make sure I had enough product ready to rock and roll, which meant a stop by the natural food store for raw sugar, coconut oil, and bees wax, and then a quick stop by the apothecary for more essential oils. Everything in my products was all-natural, the closer to nature the better. I just had to get this stupid run out of the way first. So, my plan was to run there, downtown around the city squares, pop into those two stores and then head home and get to work.

I left my truck at the marina and set out from there. It was early by my standards, about nine AM, but Seaside Days were in full effect. The carnival rides were already roaring to life and I thought long and hard about an elephant ear. Those things were the best. But I did already have a cheesecake muffin. *No, I will demonstrate some will power and start running.* In the opposite direction. As quickly as possible. However, the sidewalk sales congested the streets and had me rethinking my plan, again. *I wonder if shopping burns any calories?* It burned through the cash in my wallet, for sure. *Nope, I must move forward.*

Once I made it through the heaviest retail section of the strip, the crowds thinned out and my run picked up pace. I saw Military Mary straight ahead, doing laps around the park square. Against my better judgement, I decided to try to catch up with her and congratulate her on her win yesterday, and see if she had heard about Paulette. *Sweet sugar, that woman can run.* Either that, or my running game was seriously lacking. Probably a combination of both.

This was a terrible plan.

My calves burned and I was only about three minutes into it. Why did I want to talk to her anyway? Did I think she killed Paulette? I had a feeling Mary was a very sore loser. I lost sight of her for a few minutes and was ready to give up only to realize that she was lapping me. She came up from behind, her gait smooth and strong. *Here I am, all huffing and puffing, and there she is breathing all calm like.* I was really starting to not like her.

"Hey...congratulations...on your big...win...yesterday," I puffed out when she caught up to me.

"Thank you." Mary looked straight ahead. She picked up her pace, ready to put me behind her, but I followed suit.

"You...seemed...confident."

"Of course. One doesn't win by accident."

Uh-huh. "How...so?" *Could you slow down a bit, lady? Seriously, I'm dying here!*

Mary stopped short and I ran right into her. "Oof, sorry."

Mary looked at me like I was an idiot and then started jogging again. At least this time a little bit slower.

"You train. Winners are made, not born," she said.

"In the kitchen?" I wanted to make sure we were talking about the baking competition.

"Where else?" And then she picked up the pace again and I let her pull away.

Wow, she is ... hardcore. I had a feeling she tackled everything in life like it was a competition. I wasn't sure if that was a good thing or not. *Wonder just how far she'd go to win?*

I didn't see Mary for the rest of my run, which admittedly wasn't as long as it should have been. With exercise checked off my list, I ran, or rather walked, and completed my other two errands and was ready to get home and get to work when I spotted Mayor Potts, pacing in front of the courthouse steps. He had on a cheery yellow suit, but he looked downright distraught. His usual limp was a bit more pronounced, probably from all the extra walking he had been doing. He didn't have his cane with him, but boy, he could've sure used it. I was planning on completely ignoring him and continuing past when he made eye contact. I couldn't ignore the worry I saw there.

"Is everything okay?" I asked.

"Such dreadful news. So unfortunate," Mr. Potts said.

That it was. I thought back to the comment Mrs. J. made about he and Paulette having relations. He must have been devastated to lose someone that he cared so much about. "I'm very sorry to hear," I started to say...

"Just, the worst timing. I know how many people rely on Seaside Days for their businesses."

"Oh..." Well, there was that. Not really the *worst* of it, in my opinion.

"And the press. Of course, the local paper downplayed it, at my request, but I can't promise anything. Not when the rest of the news gets out."

"What rest?" I hadn't heard anything.

"Poisoned. That's what I've been told. Such a mess. I hope it doesn't affect turnout this weekend."

I suppose it was the mayor's job to be concerned about things like that, but I had to be honest, he was in way over his head. I hoped he didn't have anything official to do with the investigation. He probably wasn't even supposed to be talking about it.

"The farmers market, silent auction ... they all need to be big hits," he continued. "If this festival fails, I guarantee I'll lose the election to McGovern's boy." Mayor Potts scowled and then he started to pace once more. I stumbled for the right words.

"Mayor Potts," Detective Roxy called out, motioning with her finger for the mayor join her. She had just walked down the courthouse steps, annoyance stamped on her face.

I had a feeling he was about to get scolded. Personally, I was grateful for the interruption.

"Oh yes, keep it very hush-hush. I'm not supposed to be saying anything."

I was right. "Got it, and I'm sorry about your loss."

"What? Oh, yes, yes. So sad. Very heartbreaking."

He didn't look all that heartbroken, but I knew people grieved differently. I turned to leave when I heard Detective Roxy say, "Ziva, one minute." I gave an internal sigh. I didn't have time for this. My products needed to set for so many hours before they would be ready to sell tomorrow. I really needed to get a move on. I waited rather impatiently for my turn, and Detective Roxy walked over to me a moment later.

"I heard this wasn't the first dead body you've found," she said by way of introduction. Today, she had favored a pretty pink lipstick with a soft blue eyeshadow. Both look good on their own, but mixing them together was another beauty no-no. I wondered if I should've let her know that. Right now probably wasn't the best time. I got back to her question.

"No, actually it was the second. Wait, no make that the third. Last time, it was two bodies, but one murder so..." I wasn't sure if that made things better or not. *Shut up, Ziva, so you can get out of here!*

"And you just happen to keep finding these bodies?" Detective Roxy looked incredulous.

"Well, yeah, it's part of my job. Not finding dead bodies, I mean selling beauty products." I was not doing a good job of explaining myself. Probably because I was in a hurry. I tried to clarify, "I sell Beauty Secrets products, so I'm in clients' homes a lot. It just so happened that I walked in on a murder this past spring."

"And this time?" Detective Roxy asked.

"Bad luck?" I offered. *Surely, the two couldn't be related.*

Detective Roxy did the eying-me-up thing again. *So annoying.* I didn't know what she expected to find. If she didn't stop, I was about to mention her makeup faux pas.

"What can you tell me about Mrs. Birdie Jackson?"

Oh boy. Maybe we should go back to discussing the dead bodies. I wondered how close I should stick to the truth... Probably should leave out the part about Mrs. J. threatening Paulette at the bake off and being at the crime scene last night. I stuck with, "Mrs. J.'s great. If you want to know anything going on in town, she's the person to ask," which was totally true.

"Would you say she and Paulette were friends?" It was obvious Detective Roxy already knew the answer to that question. Why else would she ask?

"Er, not exactly. They'd known each other for a long time though, that I know." See, I was still being honest, just leaving out the details. You know, the parts Detective Roxy really wanted to know. Sorry, but she wasn't getting that information from me. Common knowledge or not, I never talked bad about a client, especially Mrs. J., who was also practically family.

"Listen, I've really gotta run. You know tomorrow's the big farmers market and I have a lot of work to do." I held up my two brown shopping bags. "But if you have any other questions, you can stop by there and I'll try to help you out." I didn't even wait for her to reply. I just gave a quick sorry (not sorry) and jogged off.

THE FIRST PRODUCT I needed to make was my lotion bars, as they took the longest to set. Tomorrow, I was featuring sweet orange, lavender, and my favorite—chocolate. The bars got their scents from essential oils, except for the chocolate one. That scent was curtesy of natural cocoa butter. Anytime I could include chocolate in my products, whether edible or not, I was all about it.

I had just finished pouring the bars into their molds when Aria and Christina stopped by. Holy moly. Talk about looking rough. *Is Aria still wearing her pajamas?* She wasn't the messy-hair-don't-care type. Aria usually cared. A lot. I often said she could make yoga pants look glamorous, but she was not rocking the pajama pants. Not even a little bit.

"You look horrible," I told her, holding the door open for her to walk in. Christina followed, looking like night and day with her pressed Oxford button down and penny loafers. Her braided hair was twisted up into a sophisticated French twist. I wasn't sure if Aria had even brushed her hair.

Aria walked right past me into my kitchen and began rummaging through my cupboards.

I leaned in and whispered to Christina, "Has she been like this all morning?"

"All morning." Christina plopped an accordion folder down on my kitchen counter. "And we have work to do. I need her to focus."

"Yikes." I meant that in more ways than one.

Aria rejoined us with a king-sized candy bar and took a giant bite. *Sweet sugar, something's definitely up.* The only chocolate the girl usually ate was the gourmet, eighty-five percent, dark-chocolate variety.

"Can you give us a few minutes?" I asked Christina.

Christina looked over to Aria, but she was totally zoned out, devouring her candy bar. I knew Christina didn't want to, but she wouldn't be rude either. "I suppose." Christina walked over to the living room and took a seat. I would've preferred her to walk back out the front door but, ah, whatever.

I pulled a bottle of water out of my fridge and gave it to Aria. She was going to need it to dilute her system and counter the sugar high she was about to experience. One needed to build up a tolerance before devouring a candy bar of that size. I should know, I was a professional.

"What's going on?" I semi-whispered to her.

Aria looked at me with big tears in her eyes. I made a sour face. Did I mention how much I hated it when people cried?

Aria knew that.

"Sorry." She wiped the tears away with the back of her hand and took a deep breath. I handed her a tissue from the kitchen counter and gave her a minute to compose herself.

"You good?"

She nodded.

"Okay, so what's wrong?" I asked.

"Everything!" Aria threw her hands in air and then dabbed her eyes with the tissue. "For starters, our kids hate one another." Vince had a daughter, Amelia, from a previous marriage. She was six years old, just a couple months older than Aria's son Arjun, and from what I had heard, they didn't like to share. Aria said it was like having twins who hated one another. "And Vince has to go out of town now. And did you hear about Paulette? She was poisoned. Poisoned! And you know what she ate yesterday? Mrs. J.'s cake. I can't have her make my wedding cake!"

Aria was about to lose it with the tears. I had to talk some sense into her. "Hang on a sec. Maybe Paulette was poisoned, but that doesn't mean Mrs. J.'s to blame. Who knows what else Paulette ate yesterday. Maybe it was one of the other contestants' desserts or a fast food burger gone bad. I think you're getting a little ahead of yourself."

"And you want me to chance that with my wedding cake?" Aria looked incredulous.

"You think she really poisoned Paulette? I guarantee if she did, it wasn't an accident." I slapped my hand over my mouth because both of us knew that was true. In fact, I remembered Mrs. J.'s comment from yesterday afternoon about wanting to put a little something extra in Paulette's slice of cake. "Let me talk to Mrs. J. and see what she knows. It's not like she has poison lying around her kitchen." At least, I didn't think she did. Aria didn't look convinced. "You just focus on your family, let me worry about the rest." I wasn't sure when I would have the time to worry about the rest with everything I had going on this week, but somehow, I would make it work. I sealed the deal with a smile that looked more confident than I was, and a promise to be Mrs. J.'s assistant baker on the big day. She probably wouldn't let me, but hey, no need to bring that up.

"Feel better?" Christina asked as she came back into the kitchen. Aria nodded. I wrapped her in a big hug.

"Why don't you go get a wheat grass smoothie or something like that? Treat yo' self," I said with a half laugh, even though I was mostly serious. Wheat grass made me gag, but I knew Aria loved it. "And here, take a jar of this. I'm still fine-tuning the formula, so it's not for sale yet, but it's a skin soothing cream. It should help with whatever you've got going on." I motioned to her mess of a face. I was hoping the tea tree oil and honey found in the cream would help calm her skin. A trip to the dermatologist probably wouldn't be a bad idea either.

"I'm going to finish what I'm doing here and I'll give you a call later to see how things are going. Deal?"

"Sounds good."

"Okay, don't stress. A week from now you'll be on your honeymoon, and none of this will matter. Know where you're going yet?"

"Not a clue." At least that got a smile out of her.

"Just keep thinking about that." I was totally jealous. What I wouldn't give for a vacation right about now, but with all my cash poured into my business, it was going to be a long time before that happened. *Eye on the prize*, I reminded myself.

I ushered the girls out and got back to work. The lotion bars were cooling on my coffee table, but I still had to make more of my peach passion sugar scrub and lush lemon bath bombs. So much work to do! Maybe when it was all said and done, I'd be able to take some time and pamper myself...

As it turned out, I barely had time to take a quick shower, let alone the long soak in the tub I had been envisioning, before it was time to head to my parents' house for my birthday dinner. One positive was Mrs. J. would be there. She had always been my grandma's plus one, and the invitation still stood even though my nana had earned her angel wings. If all went as planned, I'd be able to talk to Mrs. J. one-on-one and get her take on what happened to Paulette, and hopefully be able to reassure Aria that her wedding cake would be perfect.

5

*M*y parents used to live in what had been dubbed "Old Port Haven." The houses were small, the community close, and everyone mowed their own lawns. It was the type of place where kids still rode their bikes together, ran through sprinklers, and everyone looked out for one another. Since retiring, my parents wanted to focus more on traveling and enjoying their golden years than in upkeeping their house, so they moved last year into a newly constructed condo. The condo was nice, as were their neighbors, but it wasn't the same as their old digs. Apparently, I was the only one who felt that way. My mom loved her shiny new kitchen, decked out in granite and stainless steel, and my dad loved that he could fit a 55-inch television comfortably on the living room wall.

Mrs. J. might be the best baker in town, but she couldn't hold a spoon to my mom's cooking. Our Puerto Rican roots run deep, and birthdays were celebrated with food. My mom was just taking the tostones out of the oil when I walked in. The fried plantain cakes were Puerto Ricans' equivalent to French fries, only sweeter. I nabbed one off the paper towel, even though it was burning hot. I couldn't resist. My mom tried to swat my hand. "Those are for dinner!" But it was only a half attempt. I kissed her on top of the head. Being that I'm a shorty, she was the only person I could do that to.

"Don't worry, I'll save you one," I said with a smile and scooted out of striking range.

"Hi, Papa." I popped my head around the corner into the living room. My dad was sitting forward in his favorite recliner, watching "the game," which referred to anything baseball oriented.

"He's going to blow it!" he said to no one in particular, "Again! They're never going to make it to the playoffs with a bullpen that can't go deep. Cripes." My dad looked up and spotted me. "Hey, Ziva."

"Good game?"

"Every single time." I would hate to be a relief pitcher. I don't care how much money they made. Imagine that stress. *Yikes.*

I walked over to the fridge and got my dad a beer, and a bottle of red for my mom and me. Mrs. J. usually brought her own "hooch." I twisted the cap off and walked out to the living room, where I handed it to him and kissed his cheek.

"Finn with you?" he asked.

"Nope, charter, but next time..." *That is, if I tell him about it.*

Mrs. J. walked in a minute later. She was dressed in a shimmery turquoise number, my favorite color. She was killing it too. If I had dressed head to toe in the bright greenish-blue color, I'd look like a peacock.

"Mmm-mm. It smells good in here!" Mrs. J. said, greeting my mom. She was right; it did smell divine. I was thinking that had something to do with the pollo guisado simmering on the stove. The chicken stew was about as authentically Puerto Rican as you could get, or maybe it was the pork roast, pernil, just finishing up in the oven. I couldn't wait to get my hands on that crispy skin. When I walked into the kitchen, I decided that it didn't matter where my parents lived, it smelled like home.

"Mrs. J., what can you tell us today?" my dad asked, joining us in the kitchen. Mom gave him a discerning look with one eyebrow raised. *"Gossiping shouldn't be encouraged,"* I could hear her saying in my head. My dad just smiled.

"Ziva, set the table, please," my mom ordered. I did as she asked, but kept my ears open.

"Well, y'all know Paulette's dead. Good riddance, I say. Guess that means I should go to church. Speaking of which, we could use a little extra hand tomorrow night at Bingo. Ziva, you free?" Mrs. J. hollered the last part toward the dining room.

Oh no, I was not free. I just didn't know what I was going to be doing. I could see my mother just over Mrs. J.'s shoulder, fully expecting me to accept. Church was church, and you lent them a hand when they asked. It didn't matter if it was our church or not.

"It's food bingo," Mrs. J. said, reading my hesitation, as if that somehow made a difference. "You can win frozen pizzas or pot pies. Last time, I won a whole turkey, and they even let the workers take home the unclaimed prizes."

Unfortunately for me, I couldn't think up an excuse quickly enough. With Finn out of town, I didn't have any hot dates planned. I reluctantly accepted and could only hope that it wouldn't be too bad.

Dinner was served. It was all I could've dreamed of and more.

"How's the wedding plans coming?" Mrs. J. asked.

My stew went down the wrong pipe and I coughed hard. My dad laughed. I did not find it funny.

"We're not ... it's not that serious," I stammered.

"I meant Aria, sug'." Mrs. J. looked at me with the most bewildered expression and then smiled, as if she knew something I didn't.

"Oh. Right, yeah of course. Um, they're good. I mean, Aria's a bit of a stressed-out mess right now, but I think it's going to be great." *Minus the fact that she's worried you're going to poison her.* Of course, I didn't say that, but rather changed the subject. "Are you going to be at the farmers market tomorrow?"

"Wouldn't dream of missing it. Gotta sell my desserts. Although, I would've liked that champion ribbon to display on my booth. Darn Paulette. Whoops. God rest her soul and all, but she was a pain in the butt."

"What's your theory about Paulette, Mrs. J.?" My dad leaned forward to hear her take.

"Luis! Not at the dinner table!" my mom hissed, trying to hush the subject. No one listened to her.

"Well, I've been thinking, and maybe it was Humphrey," Mrs. J. said.

"The mayor?" I asked.

"Of course. If I had to listen to Paulette jibber jabber every day, I'd want to kill her too."

This got a chuckle out of my dad. My mom clearly didn't approve. "Mayor Potts is a very nice man. I hardly doubt he would kill his girlfriend," she said in a matter-of-fact voice.

"I'm not so sure," I said. "I talked to him today and he didn't seem all that upset that she was dead, but he was worried about the festival and how it would affect the turnout. So, there's that. If he was going to kill her, it probably wouldn't be during Seaside Days."

"Unless that's his cover," Mrs. J. said in a curious voice. "I guess it could've been. I don't know though... I told that to that blond bimbo, but did she listen to me? Nope." Mrs. J. looked annoyed.

"Blond bimbo? You mean detective Roxy? She visited you?" I wasn't surprised, but I had to play it off.

"Detective who?" Dad questioned.

"New detective in town," I supplied.

"New pain in the keister is what she is," Mrs. J. said.

"Birdie!" My mom was still trying to maintain some dinner table decorum.

"Listen, I don't care what her name is or where she's from. She can just hightail it outta here. Coming up to me with her attitude. I ain't having it. She needs to show me some respect."

Oh boy. I had a feeling Mrs. J. hadn't been on her best behavior. "What did she say?" I asked.

"Wanting to know what I thought of Paulette. Heard I had threatened her. I told her I'd show her a threat. Then she goes asking if she can see my cake recipe. I asked if she bumped her head. No one gets my recipe!"

My dad clapped his hands, as if this whole thing was hilarious. He had to get his amusement from somewhere, with my mom acting all hoity toity.

"You'd better be nice to her," I said.

My mom agreed, "She's the police. You need to show her some respect."

"Pssht. She better show me some respect. Mrs. Jackson don't take sass from no one." That she didn't.

"Yeah, but you gotta admit, you hated Paulette, and she ate your cake, and now she's dead. Poisoned. Mysteriously."

"I ain't got time to kill anybody. Didn't you hear me say I was selling my bake goods tomorrow? Someone's gotta frost all them cookies and pour out the pies. Besides, my back's been bothering me. I'm not about to bury anyone in the sand."

We sat in silence while we thought about it. Mrs. J. did have a point. I had more questions for her, but I didn't want to ask in front of my mom.

"So, who wants some cake?" my dad asked.

I have to admit, I was a little hesitant to eat Mrs. J.'s cake. Here I had been telling Aria not to worry about her wedding cake, when I didn't want to eat my birthday cake. I tried to pretend I was too full and planned to take it home; but let's face it, I'm never too full for cake. I did buy myself a little time with a bathroom break while everyone dug in. I figured I'd give them a ten-minute head start. That way, if things did turn south, at least one of us could call an ambulance. Of course, nothing like that happened and Mrs. J.'s cake was divine as usual. Tonight, she had made a three-layer, red-velvet cake, slathered in cream cheese frosting and topped with pecans. *Swoon.* Why she'd never written a cookbook was beyond me. Oh wait, that's right, her recipes were top secret. Minor detail. It was a shame I even had to second guess her. That alone made me want to solve this mystery. No one should ever be afraid to eat cake.

It was a good thing I wore leggings. I would need to get in two solid days of cardio to make up for all the calories I ate. It was a shame Finn was out of town. He could've lent me a hand … as a running partner, of course. Speaking of which, he would've loved my mom's cooking, especially that crispy pork. If he thought bacon was good (and who didn't?) he would've been in heaven. I sighed just thinking about it and then gave another sigh that had nothing to do with food. I was pathetic. I was missing him, and he just left this morning. What's worse is I was having a bit of guilt for not even telling him he had been invited tonight. Triple sigh.

MRS. J. HAD her goodie bag tucked under her arm and we headed out. The evening summer air smelled sweet after baking in the sun all day. I debated avoiding Main Street with all the Seaside Days' festivities, but it really was the best way back through town.

From the stop-and-go traffic, last night's drama hadn't affected the crowds. The carnival was in full swing, and the grandstand lawn was packed in anticipation of tonight's concert. Vendors were already walking the grounds, twirling glow sticks and blinking doodads. If I seriously didn't still have a ton of work to do before tomorrow, I'd be ringing up Aria to head out. We couldn't do it tonight, but a girl's night was definitely in order soon. We both needed it. Aria perhaps more than I.

"I meant to ask. Who else was close to Paulette? Besides Mayor Potts?" I asked Mrs. J. as we inched forward.

Mrs. J. chewed her lip for a moment. "Well, Suzanne Butterfield was her girlfriend. Mind you, I don't like her either. Those old biddies were two birds of a feather."

"I forgot about her... That's right, she was a judge too. What else does she do?"

"She owns Suzy-Bee Honey, you know, all those fancy honeys and what not? She makes those. Thinks she's so high-class with her honey bees."

I vaguely remembered seeing the honey for sale around town. "She live in town?"

"You thinking of paying her a visit?"

"Maybe. I need a local source of raw honey and honeycomb for my beauty line. I'm paying a fortune in shipping right now." That wasn't the real reason I wanted to know where she lived, but it was true nonetheless.

"I suppose that's all right. Her farm's off Miller Road, past Granger Bridge."

"Yeah, I know right where that's at. Thanks."

"Like I said, she and Paulette got along real well."

"What about on the opposite end, anyone dislike her as much as you?"

"Well now, that's a toughie. If I had to come up with a name, I'd say Vicki Kline."

I thought for a minute, but her name didn't register. "I don't know her."

"Well, she was a friend of theirs, I guess you could say. Quite a bit younger, but she was always following Paulette and Suzanne around. They obviously didn't like her, but she constantly wanted their approval. It's a shame she gave two licks what those other two thought of her."

"Where does she work now?"

"Well, it used to be the library, but now she's at the conservatory. She's all about flowers. A little cuckoo over them, in my opinion, obsessive really. Although, I gotta say, she's one rose that never bloomed."

I was thinking there was more to it and was surprised, for once, that Mrs. J. didn't know more. *She must be slipping.*

"What is it with you and Paulette anyway? You two used to be friends, didn't you?"

"She never was a friend, stealing from me the way she did."

"Steal?" I had never heard anything about a theft.

"My recipes!"

"What?"

"I tell you, we were going to open a bakery together back

when we were younger. I turn around one minute and the next she's opening it by herself, selling my recipes off as her own. You see what I'm saying? That's the type of woman Paulette was. It's no wonder she was murdered." Mrs. J. scowled.

I nodded and added *backstabber* to my list of Paulette's character traits. So far, that only made Mrs. J.'s motive stronger. I also thought that explained why she would never share her recipes with anyone.

"Does she still own the bakery?" I asked.

"No, she sold it, and made a pretty penny too." Mrs. J. folded her arms and settled further down in her seat.

Yeah, that would rub me the wrong way. "I see. No wonder you two didn't like one another. I heard you yesterday, too, saying you wanted to put a little extra something in her slice of cake. You'd better hope no one else heard it."

Mrs. J. gave a little chuckle and perked up a bit. "Ah, sug'. I meant a laxative. Make her get the tootsie trots in those white capris she always wore."

I laughed, even though I shouldn't have. "You would have. You totally would've, but you'd better be careful. Detective Roxy isn't messing around. You might want to, I don't know, act a little sad or something. Like maybe you'll miss her."

"Miss Paulette? Ha, that ain't happening. Of course, it would've been nice if she'd just moved away and not taken a dirt nap, but I'll take what I can get."

I raised an eyebrow and hid another smile. "And keep that to yourself, too."

6

I was so nervous Sunday morning I couldn't think straight. I'd done hundreds of beauty demos, but they were all for Beauty Secrets. This time, I was representing my own brand. When I arrived at the market, I skipped setting up for a minute to jog over to the carnival grounds and beg for a funnel cake. Surely, someone had to be working. I found a vendor, piping fresh ones out, complete with custard, powdered sugar, and hot-fudge sauce. I was in heaven and inhaled that baby. It was glorious, and the sugar buzz was just the confidence boost I needed to tackle the day.

Of course, my buzz was short lived when I reached my booth and saw Justine setting up directly across from me. *Why me?* The last time we did an event beside one another, it ended up a mess. Well, for her anyway. I thought it had been quite laughable. At least she was out of the beauty business, for now. She had a large black banner with hot pink writing that said *Puptastic Fashions*. Although, the script writing had so many loops and curls that it looked like "Pooptastic Fashions." That made me smile. If anyone was pooptastic, it was Justine. It looked like she specialized in tutus and headbands for her furry friends. She had racks and racks of little outfits set up, all color-coordinated and almost all featured tulle and sequins. Of course, she had Candy with her too. Today, the miniature poodle was dressed like a princess with a sparkly yellow satin dress and light blue tulle petticoat. Her look was complete with a little rhinestone tiara and painted pink nails.

"Breakfast?" Justine held up a dog biscuit.

"Would hate to steal yours," I said with a smile.

"Good heavens, child. What on Earth happened to your hair?" Mrs. J. startled us both.

"What? What's wrong?" Justine turned side to side, trying to inspect her own head.

"It's supposed to look like that," I remarked, knowing exactly what Mrs. J. was talking about.

"Well, it looks terrible." *Gotta love a woman who tells it like it is.*

Justine favored "chunky" highlights, which amounted to giant strips of her naturally red hair being bleached various shades of orange. I liked to believe she did it herself as no professional should ever do such a horrendous job. Justine also tended to favor volume, which, in her case, meant making her head look like a giant cheese doodle.

Justine stuck out her tongue at me because she had the maturity of a ten-year-old. I looked for something to throw at her, but then remembered I was an adult. Instead, I got back to work.

As luck would have it, Suzy-Bee Honey was setting up next to me. I didn't know Suzanne personally, but I hoped to strike up a conversation with her. She reminded me of

Christina, looking all-business in her pressed khaki Capris and a crisp white shirt. I watched her tie a black apron on that had been embroidered with her name, with a beehive next to it. She wore her blond hair in a similar style to Paulette's: bangs out of her face with a headband. And she wore a gold watch on her wrist, like Paulette. They could've passed as sisters.

"Jeffery, not there. I meant here!" I jumped a bit at her command to the younger man who was with her. He sported slim jeans and a gray polo shirt with the same logo, and was setting up signage, apparently in the wrong spot. He was tall and thin, with black wire-framed glasses. Just watching him rearrange everything, I could tell Suzanne was difficult to please. "Oh, never mind. Go get the rest of the boxes," she snapped at the poor guy. He did as he was told, as I assumed he did every day.

I looked down the row and saw Mrs. J. setting up her bakery booth just a couple down from me. I was glad we weren't right next to one another, or I would've eaten all her inventory. Thankfully, the market kicked off right about then and I was able to forget about Mrs. J.'s cupcakes.

I had put out a couple testers to let my products speak for themselves, and my strategy appeared to pay off. The lotion bars were a big hit, especially the chocolate ones. Even my lush lemon bath bombs sold well, no demo needed. After all, who didn't want to experience a colorful, fizzy bath that smelled amazing too?

The crowds picked up and I spotted several familiar faces, friends from high school, people from church; it seemed like the residents of Port Haven were in full attendance.

"Hey, Ziva, how's it going?"

I looked up to see a good-looking guy who obviously knew me, but I had no idea who he was. I hated when I couldn't place a face.

"Going well, how are you?" I played along, hoping his identity would pop into my brain.

"Doing just fine." He looked as if he was going to say something else, but then abruptly changed his mind and turned and left.

That was weird. I didn't have time to dwell on it as just then I heard Mrs. J. causing a commotion. I didn't recognize who she was arguing with, but Suzanne did.

"That Vicki Kline again. I'm not sure which one of those women are worse," she said to Jeffery.

I took a closer look. Vicki wore her dark hair in a long braid down her back. She, too, wore glasses, only her black frames were a thicker plastic. Very librarian. I highly doubted she was used to causing a ruckus.

Vicki's booth was next to Justine's, so kitty-corner from mine. I was worried Mrs. J. might be accusing her of murder, or something like that, which could've very well been the case given what Mrs. J. said about her the night before. But it turned out to be an argument over flowers. Yes, you heard me correctly. Vicki was selling a variety of potted plants and rose bushes to anyone and everyone, except for Mrs. J.

"You always kill them!" Vicki was saying. "I can't, in good conscience, sell you one."

I thought back to Mrs. J.'s porch. She did always have different flowers set out. I just thought she liked to switch it up. It never occurred to me she was killing them off.

"What do you care? They're plants. Now give me that pink one right there." Mrs. J. plucked a leaf off one and dropped it to the ground. I thought Vicki was going to blow a gasket.

"They're *my* plants."

Mrs. J. plucked off another leaf.

"Don't touch them again."

Pluck.

"Birdie Jackson, you're impossible! Now get!"

"I'll get once I have my plant."

"That is not happening. Now don't make me call the police."

"You're going to call the cops over a plant?"

Vicki reached for her cell phone.

"Oh, go sit on a rose bush, you nut." Mrs. J. batted her hand toward her. "Humph. See if I donate to the conservatory anymore, with the way their employees treat me." Mrs. J. said the last part mostly to herself. I could tell she was in a bad mood, and I wasn't sure it had all that much to do with Vicki.

"How's it going, Mrs. J.?" I was surprised she had left her baked goods in the first place.

"This here's been real disappointing. Haven't sold a single pie, cupcake, cookie, you name it. It's been downright insulting. Shame on all of you!" Mrs. J. shouted to the passersby, causing a couple people to jump and maybe a baby cry (hard to tell with the little ones). I had been too busy to notice how bad her business had been, but now that I looked around, I realized people were clearly avoiding her.

"That's ridiculous. Send some of your sweets my way and I'll set them out on my table."

"Good idea. Thanks, sug'. I'll be right back." Mrs. J. brought an assortment of desserts over and I gladly displayed them. I was surprised by how much table space I had, but then again, I shouldn't have been, seeing that I was almost out of inventory. Hopefully, I'd have the same luck with Mrs. J.'s baked goods.

I saw Mayor Potts making his way through the crowd, doing his mayor shtick: shaking hands, chuckling, telling a joke to whomever would listen. *Could he be a killer? He doesn't look like one.* I watched as he played an impromptu game of peek-a-boo with a baby. *No, definitely not a killer.*

"Morning, Mr. Mayor," I said when he stopped by.

"Well, don't those just look delicious." Mr. Potts eyed up the tuxedo cupcakes. They were chocolate cupcakes dipped in ganache and then topped with white cream frosting. Sounds amazing, right?

"They are. I love them." Well, I was sure I would once I ate one. I had already planned on buying a baker's dozen from Mrs. J. Those were a personal favorite of Finn's. Oh, never mind. What was I thinking? They would be stale by the time he got back.

My mind went back to the sale and making Mrs. J. some cash. "Do you want to sample one?"

"Oh yes, yes I would. That would be wonderful." Mr. Potts took a healthy bite and I found myself a little jealous. I was thinking I should try one too. That is, until I remembered my delicious funnel cake from just a couple hours ago. I needed to show *some* self-control, especially with how horrendous my eating habits had been. And working out? Yeah, that hadn't been happening either. *Okay, self-control starts NOW.*

"What do you think? Would you like to purchase a few?" I thought Mr. Potts was about to say yes. He opened his mouth, but nothing came out. My smile vanished. *Oh my gosh, is he choking? What in the world is going on?*

"Are you okay?" No sooner were the words out of my mouth did his eyes roll into the back of his head and he crashed onto the ground.

Sweet sugar. I killed the mayor.

As it turned out, he wasn't dead. But he wasn't doing well either. Once the ambulance left and the chaos settled, I found myself face to face with Detective Roxy, again. *Oh boy, here we go again.*

Detective Roxy had on a pair of skinny jeans, a pink tank top, and pink Converses. I liked her style. Except for her makeup. Today, everything was pink—her lipstick, eyeshadow, blush. The explosion of pink on her face, plus her outfit, was just way too much. I couldn't think of a polite way to clue her in that she looked like a giant ball of cotton candy.

Unfortunately, Detective Roxy wasn't here to talk about her style, or lack thereof. She got right to work. "Pretty convenient you found Paulette, and now this business with the mayor." Convenient wasn't the word I would've used. She waited for me to explain.

"I was just helping out a friend. Her business was slow and I thought I'd give her a hand. I let her set up her baked goods on my table."

"Would this friend be a Mrs. Birdie Jackson?"

"It would." I eyed the crowd, looking for Mrs. J., but I couldn't spot her. I didn't want to throw her under the bus, but I didn't want to lie. The fact was Mr. Potts ate one of her cupcakes and then keeled over, and no one else had eaten any.

"Is he going to be okay?" Detective Roxy knew who I meant.

"Not sure yet." I had no idea if she'd tell me the truth, even if she did know. Detective Brandle would've.

"Let me know how else I can help. I've never seen anything like that," I told her.

Detective Roxy seemed to see that I was sincere. "Tell

your friend to give me a call. She seems to have disappeared."

I looked around again, but the detective was right. *Oh great.* Next thing I knew, there'd be an APB out for Mrs. J. *What was she thinking? Unless she's turned into a psychopathic killer...* I told Detective Roxy I would keep her updated, and turned to get back to work.

"What are you selling?" Detective Roxy asked.

"I started my own beauty line. All my products are hand-made with natural ingredients like honey, coconut oil, beeswax, essential oils, things like that. So, they're super moisturizing, and they smell delectable."

"Really?"

Finally, an opening.

Detective Roxy left my booth with several of my products, including a few lotion bars, lip balms, and bath bombs. I also told her about Beauty Secrets and slipped her a catalog. I couldn't do anything about today's pink fiasco, but I could offer her a mini makeover, which is exactly what I did.

"Hi, I couldn't help but overhear you talking. I would love to try out one of your lotion bars. My hands get so dry from working in the dirt." Vicki, the plant lady, stood before me, completely shy, with not an ounce of anger left.

"Oh yeah, um, that was my last one. But ... I have an extra bar in my purse that you're more than welcome to." It was from a previous batch, but still worked great.

"If you're sure?"

"Absolutely. This a lemon scent I was experimenting with. You'll have to let me know what you think." Vicki took the bar and sniffed it. "Sweet, huh? All you need to do is hold it in your hands and let it melt just a little, then rub it in. Your hands will be super soft and hopefully protected a bit from the soil."

"Thanks, I'll definitely give it a try."

"You really like plants," I said. Vicki blushed slightly. I had a tough time believing she was the same person shouting moments ago.

"I do. It's a hobby turned passion."

"That's awesome. That's how I feel about my business. You need to do what you love."

"Exactly. I used to work a day job, but once I made time to focus on me, I discovered that I loved botany. Plants are fascinating."

"You work at the conservatory?"

"I do."

"I love the gardens there. So beautiful, with all the different themes. The orchids are my favorite." They didn't usually make me sneeze.

"Which ones? Cymbidiums? Phalaenopsis?"

"Er, the purple ones? Sorry, I'm terrible with names." *And with plants in general.* Vicki probably wouldn't be so nice to me if she knew how many plants I'd killed in my day.

"Hold on." Vicki ran to her table and rushed back to me. "If you want to learn, I teach a couple classes." She placed a flier in my hand. The conservatory offered *Gardening Basics, Trimming 101, Eat it!,* and *Poisonous Plants in your Garden.*

"Wow, thanks so much. I know I need to learn more, especially in this line of work." My holistic knowledge was very basic.

"Anytime. Hi, Jeffery." Vicki turned her attention to whom I gathered was Suzanne's husband. He looked up and smiled.

"Jeffery, are you done yet?" Suzanne snapped. It was bizarre. I had watched Suzanne all morning. She seemed so nice to everyone, except Jeffery. People seemed to genuinely like her too. She just hated her husband and I wondered why. I couldn't help it; I was terribly nosey. *Maybe I can ask Mrs. J. about it ... if she hasn't fled the country yet.*

"I'll talk to you later," he said to Vicki.

She nodded. "Hi, Suzanne."

Suzanne completely ignored her. It was kind of sad, but I let it go.

Even after almost killing the mayor and Mrs. J. running away, my morning had gone well. Serenity Now was officially out in the world and people seemed to love my products as much as I did. I couldn't wait to tell Finn. I thought about all the ways I could celebrate. Of course, that made me think of Finn again, but since he was gone, mint chocolate chip ice cream would have to do. I was ready to pack it up and call it a success when trouble popped up.

"Ziva, can you look at this?"

"What's up?" I picked my head up from under the table. I was just gathering my things. One of my first clients from the morning had stopped back over. Her hands and forearms had the lightest red rash.

"It just itches. I have no idea what's going on."

"What the...? Are you allergic to honey or orange essential oil?"

"I don't think so."

"The only other ingredients are beeswax, shea butter, and coconut oil."

My client shook her head. "I've never had anyone have a reaction before." No sooner were the words out of my mouth did I notice two more clients headed my way, both scratching their palms and arms. *Don't panic.*

But it only got worse.

I started apologizing and handing out refunds left and right. I had no idea what had gone wrong or why so many people were having a negative reaction. Then, I looked over at Justine, laughing her head off. I had no idea what she had done, but I'd guarantee this was her fault and she was going to pay.

Unfortunately, Justine took off before I could have words with her. But I knew where she lived.

7

I spent an extra hour apologizing to everyone and offering to somehow make it right. At that moment, all I could think about was proving Justine's guilt and having her issue a public apology. I was ready to call the police and have an official investigation launched, but it turned out I didn't have to.

I had stopped back home to change my clothes and gather my thoughts before heading over to Justine's. I figured I needed a minute to clear my head before I went and did something stupid, like bash Justine in the head. When I pulled into my spot behind the antiques shop, I saw Detective Roxy waiting for me.

"Long time no see," I said.

Detective Roxy held out her palms for me to see. They were as pink as the rest of her.

"Son of a—. Not you too." I closed my eyes and growled inside. Maybe Detective Roxy could go with me to Justine's … to keep me from murdering her. I invited Detective Roxy up and shared my suspicions on what had happened.

"Do you have any more product left?" she asked.

"I didn't, but I do now thanks to all the returns." I handed a box over to her. "Seriously, whatever she did might just have ruined me, my reputation anyway. I'm not sure how I'll be able to fix this." Justine had done a lot of horrible things to me over the years, like egging the inside of my locker in middle school, but this ranked right up there as the worst.

"Let me have our guys take a look at this and see what we can find. Honestly, it reminds me of what it was like when I got poison ivy camping a few years ago."

"Poison ivy? Great. Let me know what type of legal charges I can file because, believe me, I will be filing them." Not sure it would be enough. I was already going to have to do a whole rebranding strategy and tell Mrs. DeVine what had happened. That wasn't a phone call I was looking forward to.

I then thought back to this morning with the mayor, and something bothered me about the whole Mrs. J. angle. I finally knew what it was. "Hey, listen, I know Mrs. J.'s on your radar, and I get that, I do; but I forgot to tell you, she baked two cakes on Friday. One for me and one for the competition, and no one else got sick."

"You're assuming it was an accident."

"Well yeah, I mean Mrs. J.'s not one to go around poisoning people. Her baking is legendary, and it's a point of pride for her. I can't see her ruining her reputation. Not only that, but what's her motive? Even if she didn't like Paulette, why poison the mayor?" *If that is in fact what happened.*

"I don't know, but I'm working on it."

I was afraid of that.

◇

DETECTIVE ROXY LEFT and I didn't have even five minutes to myself before Aria walked in. She was a crying mess. As in mascara running down her face, swollen eyes, runny nose, mess. My usual discomfort set in. Did I mention how much I absolutely hated crying? And Aria had a puppy with her. A poodle. At least I think that's what it was. The poor pup had been dyed shocking pink, and it looked like someone had colored in black eyebrows on him.

"What in the world is going on, girl?" I took the puppy from her arms and searched frantically for a tissue. Aria plopped down on my couch. Cue the hiccupping. My poor bestie couldn't even get the words out. I thought for a minute that her wedding had been called off, but that didn't explain the puppy.

"Here." I handed the tissue box to her. Worry set in that something serious had happened, like to one of the kids. "Arjun? Amelia?"

"They're...fine. Well...they hate each...other, but they're fine."

Whew. "Vince?"

"Ffff-ine."

M-kay. I stared at her for a moment. "You're killing me here. Wait! Someone didn't die, did they?"

Aria shook her head.

More waiting. I talked to the puppy for a minute, "What's your name, little guy?" The pink puff ball licked up my neck and tried to nibble at my ears. I held him up in front of me. "This isn't your fault, is it?"

"I just can't!" Aria finally said. Cue more crying.

"Honey, you're going to have to elaborate."

"The kids, the wedding, it's all a mess!"

"What did the kids do now?"

"They hate each other so much. Arjun cut off all of Amelia's doll's hair."

"At least it wasn't Amelia's. Am I right?"

"Don't give him any ideas. Then Vince had a puppy delivered for them, thinking it would bring them closer together."

"And it didn't?"

"Hardly. Amelia was mad that he's a boy, so she dyed him pink, and then Arjun was mad that he was pink so he drew on the eyebrows to make him look *fierce*."

"Oh boy."

"Meanwhile, Vince never ran any of it by me and I'm terribly allergic." Aria sneezed right on cue. I could relate to the allergies. Flowers were my usual trigger. Spring time was brutal for me.

"To top it all off, the hotel called this morning and someone pulled the fire alarm at last night's wedding. The ballroom has water damage, and who knows if it'll be fixed by Friday." She sobbed again.

Okay, that was all pretty rough. I tried to decide whose day had been worse—mine or hers?

"But at least you didn't kill anyone," I said with a half-smile.

Aria stopped crying. "Wait, What?!"

"Okay, so I didn't kill anyone, but I may have poisoned the mayor, or make that Mrs. J. did." I went on to explain the whole cupcake catastrophe.

"After all that, it looks like Justine struck again, with my clients breaking out in horrible rashes. So yeah, that was a disaster. Just wait until my mom hears. She'll need a Xanax. Dad will be disappointed he missed it all."

At least Aria had finally stopped crying.

"So, now what are we going to do?" I asked.

Spoke too soon. The tears threatened to spill out of Aria's eyes again.

"Don't do it, girl. I'm serious." *I thought we were past the crying.*

"I can't keep Captain Jack," she said.

"Who?"

Aria pointed to the pink puppy, who had just peed on my floor mat and was now chewing on my Converses.

"I don't want to take him to the shelter. He's such a sweetheart. None of this is his fault."

"Okay, leave the fluff ball with me and I'll find him a home." I sounded more confident than I felt. I was getting good at doing that lately. "Don't worry about your reception yet. Let's give them a day to clean up, and then we'll go check it out."

"Christina already has a list of alternate venues."

"Of course, she does." *Don't roll your eyes.* I gave my bestie a tight hug and promised her that it would all get sorted out. It might take a family therapist and a trip to Disney World to help with the kids, but in the end, it would all work out. Aria and Vince loved each other too much to not find a way.

Aria left and I looked over at Captain Jack. *Poor little guy.* He started walking around in a circle and I was a second too late to realize he was about to take a poo. *Yuck. Okay, time to reorder my priorities.* I picked up the pooch. "First up, find a nice home for you, cutie pie. Then go beat the beans out of Justine."

Turned out, I didn't have to reorder my priorities. I hated

Justine, but she did love her puppies, and they seemed to love her. I hoped we could make a deal.

Justine Martin had been married too many times to keep count. It was somewhere around six or seven, if I cared to think about it at all. She had made a habit out of marrying well, and therefore, had accumulated enough wealth to be an official royal pain in the butt.

I was big enough to admit that her red brick, colonial, two-story house with its circle driveway and plethora of windows was beautiful, although completely impractical for a single woman living alone. Her kitchen might have more square footage than my entire apartment, but I was betting all those empty bedrooms made it awfully lonely. I'd take my quaint little space any day.

I rang her bell and Captain Jack and I waited for her to answer. Not even two seconds later, a man wearing a tan vest with Bermuda shorts answered the door. I took a step back to look at the address again. I was at the right house. *Maybe Justine married again?*

"Hi, I'm looking for Justine. Is she home?"

"Miss Justine has requested not to be disturbed this afternoon."

Miss Justine? I almost snorted. "Who are you?"

"I'm sorry, ma'am. I am Withers. If you'll so kindly tell me your name, I will let the lady of the house know that you were here."

Lady of the house? Pshaw. More like lady of the night, and when did Justine get a butler?

"So, what, is your boss lady too scared to come to the door?" I tried to look past him into the house, but didn't see anything. Withers closed the door and stepped out onto the porch, causing Captain Jack and me to take a step back.

"I'm sorry, ma'am, but you're going to have to leave."

"Aw, now don't be like that. Look, I even brought an adorable little puppy." I held up Captain Jack. Okay, so he looked a little ridiculous with the pink fur and black eye brows, but under all that, he was a total cutie. Withers didn't look impressed.

I debated for a second what to do. I could just hand Captain Jack to Withers and jump in my truck and take off. I knew Justine was an animal lover, but I got the feeling Withers wasn't. For all I knew, he'd call the pound and have them come get Captain Jack without saying a word to Justine, seeing that she didn't want to be disturbed and all. Or worse, he could just leave Captain Jack on the porch. It would've been great if Justine had answered the door and I could've made a deal. Something like: you publicly admit your wrongdoing today and apologize to all my customers, and in return I'll give you this adorable puppy. That was my original plan. Now I was standing in front of Mr. Grumpy Gus, going nowhere fast.

I stared at Withers, trying to get a better read on him. "Any way you can take this little guy to Justine and ask her to come to the door?"

"I'm sorry, ma'am. Not today. Now, if you will..." Withers took another step forward. I took another step back. "Thank you. Have a nice day." Withers dismissed us and went back inside.

"Well that didn't work," I said to Captain Jack.

Now it was on to Plan B.

aptain Jack and I did a little shopping before heading to see my parents. I had no idea what type of food he ate or what toys he liked, so we bought an assortment of goodies. Turned out, puppy shopping was kind of fun. It wasn't the same as shoe shopping, but didn't cost as much either. Captain Jack even got a peanut butter biscuit for being a good boy, to go with my peanut butter cup. We both deserved a treat. The only thing better than chocolate was peanut butter with chocolate.

My dad was where I knew I'd find him, sitting in his spot, watching "the game" when I walked in. It was the same place you'd find him every Sunday afternoon. My mom met the girls for brunch, and my dad got to veg out in front of the TV in peace and quiet. Talk about relationship goals. Finn was a Sports Center fan himself.

"Hi, Papa." I greeted my dad with a kiss on the cheek and placed Captain Jack in his lap. He didn't even flinch, just started petting the pup's head. Not sure if it was a testament to his laid-back attitude or a lifetime of my shenanigans, but even a pink poodle didn't faze him.

"Heard you tried to kill the mayor," my dad said nonchalantly.

"Ah, that was quick. What did Mom say?"

"She went to church."

"Sounds about right. For the record, I didn't try to kill him. It was Mrs. J.'s cupcake that did it. By the way, you haven't seen her, have you? She took off without talking to the police." My dad laughed. "Dad, seriously, you don't think Mrs. J. would kill someone, do you?"

"Not on purpose."

"Not even Paulette?"

"Not even her. Mrs. J.'s bark is worse than her bite. Kind of like this little guy here."

"Captain Jack," I stated. "Vince got him for the kids, but Aria's allergic. I'm looking for a home for him. I was hoping you could puppy sit. I've got bingo tonight." I could've totally skipped it, but I was hoping Mrs. J. would show and I could find out what in the world she was thinking.

"You know I don't mind. Your mom's going to have a fit though."

I smiled and inched toward the door. "Which is why I'm outta here. Just tell her I'll be back in a couple hours. I left a can of food on the counter for him. Oh, and watch out for when he does the circle thing. Love you."

"Honey!" I heard my dad call as I slipped out the door.

WITH CAPTAIN JACK taken care of, I was able to run a quick errand before heading over to First Baptist. I couldn't get Mayor Potts out of my mind, seeing him pass out like that this morning left an icky feeling in my stomach. I was hoping to pop up to the hospital and see how he was doing. Maybe even poke my head in and apologize, even though I did nothing wrong.

I must've been awfully worried about the mayor because the only thing I hated worse than crying, was hospitals. Truth be told, it wasn't just concern that dragged me there, but also the thought that maybe Mrs. J. was somehow responsible. I know I had defended Mrs. J. in public, but truthfully, I was having second thoughts. Was it possible this could all just be a horrible accident? Mrs. J. was getting up there in years. I knew her vision wasn't as great as it used to be, just watching her squint to read my Beauty Secrets catalogs told me that. Maybe she mistook cyanide for sugar? I had to admit it was a possibility. Her going MIA like this morning wasn't helping either. *She had better show up for bingo.*

I was still thinking about Mrs. J. when I walked into the hospital waiting area and saw Suzanne Butterfield sitting there. She paced in front of the fish tank, staring off into space, until she saw me.

"Oh, hi Ziva."

I stopped, taken back that—one, she knew me; and two, she was being nice.

"Are you here for Mayor Potts?" I asked.

"I am. He and I are good friends. I've been worried about him all afternoon. I couldn't sit around the house waiting any longer."

"Yeah, I've been thinking about him too."

"What happened? I just saw him on the ground."

"You know, one minute he was eating and then the next, BAM, passed out."

"It's that horrible Birdie Jackson. This is all her fault!"

Suzanne started pacing again. "I told the detective how much she hated Paulette, and now she's gone after the mayor. They need to lock her up before she hurts anyone else."

I knew Suzanne was no friend of Mrs. J.'s, so it didn't surprise me that she felt this way. "Have you heard anything? Maybe this has nothing to do with Mrs. J." Like, maybe the mayor had a bad heart or a heat stroke. The guy was always wearing suits and bow ties in ninety-degree weather. Not the smartest wardrobe choice, in my opinion.

"Oh, there's Maryanne now." Suzanne rushed over to her. I hung back. I had no idea who Maryanne was, but my guess was she was family, maybe Mayor Pott's daughter or niece.

The two women had an animated conversation, Suzanne's loud voice making it easy to eavesdrop. "No! Poisoned? The same as Paulette? I knew it!" she exclaimed.

Suzanne rounded on me and I braced for her to let me have it. After all, I was friends with Mrs. J. and had given Mr. Potts the cupcake. I held out hope that there was some sort of crazy coincidence going on.

Suzanne totally deflated and practically fell into my arms.

Oomph. I did not expect that.

"First Paulette, and now Humphrey. I just can't take it," she said, sobbing. I tensed up and awkwardly patted her back. I looked up to Maryanne, who also had tears in her eyes. *Just shoot me now.* Why couldn't they just hug one another and let me scoot out of here? Whenever anyone cried in front of me, my goal was to get them to stop as soon as possible. I was all for having a good cry, but in the comfort of your own home, wearing pajamas, and preferably with chocolate in hand. This whole crying-in-public bit was just too much for me. I spotted a box of tissues on the end table and let go of Suzanne so I could hand them both a few.

"Sorry," Suzanne said.

"No, it's okay." A total lie.

Suzanne blew her nose softly into the tissues, and Maryanne dabbed her eyes.

"So, is he okay?" I asked Maryanne.

"He will be. He's weak, but recovering."

"That's a relief." Honestly, I wasn't sure he would be, seeing the way he went down. I shuddered. "They're sure he was poisoned though?"

"Grayanotoxins," Suzanne said, rejoining the conversation.

"Graya-whata?" I asked.

"Grayanotoxins. They're found in plants and in the cake Paulette ate. They found it in my uncle's blood too," Maryanne said.

Sweet sugar. I didn't think Maryanne knew I was the one that gave her uncle the cupcake, and I wasn't about to tell her. Mrs. J. had a lot of explaining to do, like how poison kept getting into her baked goods, that was if I could find her. I knew I wouldn't be the only one looking for her.

"Tell your uncle I'm thinking about him, and we'll figure out what's going on." I gave Maryanne's arm a little squeeze and left my goodbye at that, not even telling her my name. I had a feeling Suzanne would fill her in when I walked out. Hopefully, Maryanne wouldn't hate me. Between poisoning the mayor and my beauty disaster, I was betting a lot of people were cursing my name that day.

∾

I LEFT the hospital and drove to First Baptist. *Mrs. J. had better be there.* The church hall was packed with rows of folding tables with just about every spot taken. The women sat ready to roll with their cards and colored dabbers in front of them. A flat-screen television was set up behind the stage. It showed a blank bingo card while the words "Welcome to Bingo!" scrolled across the bottom. I didn't know bingo was so serious.

Unfortunately, it turned out that Mrs. J. was not there, and by *helping out*, she meant me running prizes from the back-kitchen freezer out to the winners, which happened at an alarming rate. Those ladies didn't mess around. Had I realized this, I would've dressed more appropriately. A tank top and jean shorts was not cutting it. I needed a winter coat and some Uggs. Maybe earmuffs and mittens too. Winter gear was in serious short supply here. Of course, everyone was talking about Paulette and Mayor Potts, and speculating who had it out for the couple. I was able to pick up bits and pieces as I worked the room. Was it a political foe? The mayor was up for reelection and Whip McGovern was said to be a worthy opponent. Young, ambitious, a definite threat. Paulette's ex-husband, Randy Berger, was also thrown out. Word was her divorce had been a nasty one and her ex hated Humphrey. I, for one, was happy to hear another angle besides "Mrs. J. the homicidal baker," although there were plenty who thought she was to blame. *She really should've come tonight.*

I took a break from freezer duty to warm up outside. The heat felt glorious. I looked at my phone and saw a text from my mom, wondering when I'd be back for Captain Jack. Actually, it was more like, *"Come get your dog."* I had a missed call from her as well. I text back that I was still at bingo and I'd be there soon. The woman couldn't be mad, seeing that I was at church. I tried Mrs. J.'s number next, but she didn't answer. I said a quick prayer to my nan to watch over her best friend, and I headed back inside.

Military Mary nabbed me before I could make it back to the kitchen. "Have a seat," she ordered.

It took a second to realize she was talking to me. She had a least a twenty bingo cards displayed before her several dabbers. She put two cards in front of me and handed me a dabber. I stared at her for a minute. It wasn't like I didn't know how to play; I just hadn't planned on it.

She ran those cards like a boss. "Where is your friend?" she asked, her eyes never stopped scanning her cards. It was a bit unnerving.

"Not sure. She's probably just at home, tired. It's been a couple of exciting days." *Did that sound lame?* It was the best I could do, seeing that I had no idea where she was, and I was wondering the exact same thing.

"Well, tell her to keep a lookout. Something hinky's going on here." Dab, dab, dab.

"You think so?"

"I know so. Always trust your gut." Again with the dabbing.

"So, you don't think it's Mrs. J.?"

"Nope, never did." Mary started dabbing my cards as well. "But someone's working really hard to make it seem that way. Best to stay vigilant."

"Got it."

"You too." Dab, dab, dab.

"I will." I hadn't any reason to worry about my safety, but maybe I should start. Killers seemed to be drawn to me. "You know anything about this Whip character, or Paulette's ex-husband?" I asked.

"I know they both have something to gain, and that's a

good place for the police to start." I hadn't thought of it that way, but that made sense. "A good detective always looks to see who benefits," Mary said, reading my mind. "People don't go around killing people unless they have something to gain."

Did Mrs. J. have something to gain? *A championship title*, I thought to myself. How bad did she want it? I then looked at my bingo partner. *How bad had Mary wanted it?* I didn't know either answer.

"You have a bingo, dear," Mary said, snapping me out of my thoughts.

That I did.

"BINGO!" Mary hollered on my behalf and pointed down at me. I said goodbye to her and stood up to collect my prize.

I took my spumoni ice cream and drove back across town to my parents' place. *Maybe I could use the sweet treat to butter up my mom.* The chocolate, pistachio, and cherry ice cream really wasn't my thing; it had fruit and nuts in it. I was still holding out for the mint chocolate chip that I had at home. But my mom would love it.

MY DAD WAS WALKING Captain Jack when I pulled into their driveway. Hopefully, the pup had been on his best behavior. I took the chicken route and exchanged Captain Jack for the ice cream and headed back home, totally avoiding my mother.

"Scaredy-cat," my dad had hollered after me as I backed down the driveway. I waved and smiled. He was so right.

Twilight was approaching. I wanted to drive by Mrs. J.'s house to see if she was home, but I also wanted to get back home before it was totally dark out. I took Mary's advice to heart. This wasn't my first rodeo. My security routine had turned lax the last couple of months, but it was time to start being paranoid again.

I drove straight home and got Captain Jack and myself secured for the night. He seemed content as could be once he commandeered my couch pillows. It would take more than a comfy pillow to calm me. I loaded up a bowl with three scoops of my beloved mint chocolate chip ice cream and started tooling around online. I found out that Paulette's ex husband, Randy Berger, owned a small appliance repair store on the south side of town. I saved the store's address into my phone with a promise to check it out tomorrow. I obviously knew he was divorced, but that was the only record I could find in the county clerk database. No other marriages, or any children for that matter, came up when I ran additional searches.

Next, I Googled "Whip McGovern". He was handsome, with dark hair and broad shoulders. He looked more like an athlete than a politician, also younger than I had expected. I ran a quick background check on him, returning nothing significant, no college degrees, business licenses or marriages. Only thing I really found were about a dozen different recent headshots. The man really seemed to love the camera, and probably himself. There wasn't much to note on his campaign website either, just the usual economic promises of yesteryear. I would have to dig deeper if I wanted to find out what he was really like. I made a note to find out who his friends were, or better yet, his enemies.

It looked like tomorrow morning would be busy. With a game plan, I hoped to sleep better that night. Even if it was alone. I wondered what Finn was doing. It freaked me out thinking of him bobbing around out there in the middle of the ocean. It didn't seem to bother him one bit. I supposed that was the important part; he loved his job. Still, I'd feel better when he was back on dry land or doing day trips. These crazy weeklong trips of his were going to drive me batty.

9

*M*y phone woke me from a delicious dream that I did not want to end. I sighed, still thinking about Finn, and reached over to my nightstand to grab my phone. It was a county number. My heart rate picked up. Last time I received a call from a county line, it was Aria in jail.

"Sug', you there?" Mrs. J. asked.

"Don't tell me—"

"That Detective's gone and arrested me!"

I was not surprised. "What happened?"

"Well, I may have been buying a bus ticket to get out of Dodge. You know, until this mess all blew over."

"That's not suspicious or anything. You know murder's not something that just blows over."

"Hush now. That Miss Priss said she just wanted to ask me a few questions, but I knew better. I told her to get lost."

"That all?" Sarcasm dripped from my words.

"I might have also threatened her with a little voodoo magic. Just a bit. It's in my blood, you know."

"Awesome." I wasn't sure what charges Mrs. J. was being held on. It sounded like Detective Roxy had a few to work with.

"You gotta help me, honey girl. This whole place is run by a bunch of fools."

"Keep that to yourself. I'm already working on it. You just behave and let your lawyer do the talking." I was hoping to turn something up with Randy or Whip and set Detective Roxy down the right path. It sounded like most of her efforts right now were focused on getting something to stick on Mrs. J. I already tried to tell her that was a waste of time, but I understood following the evidence. I intended to follow the motivation. Like Mary said, who had the most to gain?

Mrs. J. grumbled about not needing a lawyer, but I put the kibosh on that. "You like orange? Then just keep talking. If not, then be on your best behavior."

I couldn't solve this murder soon enough.

I HUNG up with Mrs. J. and took Captain Jack out to do his thing. He didn't pee, poo, or chew on anything throughout the night, so I considered that a success. He did however sleep plastered to my side. Surprisingly, I was okay with this. The pup and I had more in common than I originally gave him credit for, like a love of shopping and sleep. Finn might've been an early riser, but Captain Jack seemed to like to stay in bed for morning cuddles. This whole "man's best friend" thing was new to me, as my mom didn't allow any pets in the house. Well, the rule used to be: if it could be under water for five minutes and still be alive, I could have it. She probably had a goldfish in mind. However, one day I found and brought home a baby alligator instead (what? I'm a southern girl) and that put an end to that.

I had a little bit of time until Randy's appliance shop opened, so I took a nice hot shower and doubled up with my mint deep-conditioning treatment and orange zest body scrub. I hadn't told Mrs. DeVine what happened yesterday and the more I thought about it, the more I decided it would be best to have some answers first. If I could solve this little mystery, I could move forward with my business. Just another thing to think about. Speaking of business, I remembered that I was supposed to have a Beauty Secrets product shipment delivered on Saturday. I may be focused on my own beauty line, but Beauty Secrets was still my bread and butter. I had a home party booked for the following night and unless those products showed up first thing this morning, I'd have to put in a rush order and pay for overnight shipping. When I got out of the shower, I brought up my email and clicked through my inbox until I found what I was looking for—my shipping confirmation. A quick track of the package confirmed it had been delivered on Saturday, just as planned, only I had no idea where it was. I guess it was possible that someone could've stolen it. We did have a ton of extra visitors in town with Seaside Days this past weekend. Although, most people didn't walk behind the stores. It was mostly employee and tenants that parked back here, but I couldn't rule that out.

I ran downstairs to see if it had accidentally been dropped off to the antiques shop. It wouldn't have been first time if it had ended up there.

"Morning, Kathleen," I said to the shop's owner when I walked in. She was in the front window arranging a glass display. "Don't put that out, I want it." She had the most beautiful Murano glass vases that I had to have. The pink swirled glass would look perfect on my mantel.

"It's yours. What about these?" She held up a crystal champagne flute with rose gold stems. Aria would love them and I did still need to get her a wedding gift.

"Sold. Now stop showing me stuff," I said with a smile. Kathleen knew just what I liked, and I could spend way too much time and money browsing her inventory. I always found too many things that I loved and had to have. If I was looking for a rug, I'd come out with a tea set, a vintage sign, and a rug. Just like today. I don't know why I thought it would be any different.

"Hey, my Beauty Secrets order didn't by chance get dropped off here on accident, did it?"

Kathleen thought for a second. "Nope, haven't seen anything. I can call Mary and see if she saw it. She closed yesterday."

"No, this would've been delivered on Saturday."

"Then I don't think we have it. Sorry."

"Shoot, that sucks. Well, at least you did help me find the perfect wedding present for Aria. She's seriously going to love these flutes." *I* seriously loved them.

"Well, you're welcome then. I'll let you know if your shipment shows up too."

"Thanks, yeah, keep an eye out. My shipping confirmation shows that it was delivered on Saturday, so if you don't have it, I'm guessing it was stolen."

"Are you getting into trouble again?" Kathleen semi-joked. My spring had been quite eventful.

"Gosh, I hope not." In reality, it was more like, *aren't I always*?

"Let us know if you need anything. Feel free to have your shipments sent here and I'll sign for them."

"Thanks for the offer. That's a good idea. I'll do that." This is what the town of Port Haven was all about—neighbors helping neighbors. Not neighbors killing neighbors and burying them on the beach. I said goodbye to Kathleen and set off to find out who hadn't gotten that memo.

10

*C*aptain Jack and I left my apartment just after ten o'clock. I wasn't brave enough to ask my parents to watch him again and, without a crate, there was no way he was having free reign of my place. My start had been delayed as it took a little bit longer than I'd expected to put that rush order in, but I had to do that first - either that, or cancel the party, which I really didn't want to do. If Serenity Now tanked before taking off, I'd need every Beauty Secrets client I could get. Thankfully, my shipments came with insurance, so if the package never showed, I'd at least be able to file a claim. Until then, I ordered enough trial-sized lipsticks, nail polishes, and promo packs to get me through tomorrow. I tried to always have the latest deal on hand. I learned early on that if clients could see it—or better yet, try it—then they would buy it. I'd like to think that my missing products were the result of some shipping snafu, but I knew better. I swore if Justine was behind this, she would pay. Instead of waiting around to see what other stunts she would pull, I also ordered a wireless Wi-Fi camera and a few door sensors online that I could monitor with my cell phone. Extra security was smart all around.

RB Appliance Repair was in a strip mall wedged between a second-hand retail shop and a Chinese restaurant. If the interview was a bust, at least I could grab some Lo Mein for lunch. Captain Jack sniffed his nose out the window and I knew he approved of the plan.

Randy Berger was a bear of a man. Grizzly beard, two hundred and sixty pounds, at least six foot five. He looked as solid as they came. But I was thinking that all wasn't as it seemed. Maybe it was his red-rimmed eyes or the Cary Grant movie playing on his little television in the background, but there was more to Mr. Berger than what first impressions led you to believe. He hummed to himself while he worked on the inside of a window air conditioner. Captain Jack wiggled in my arms. I wasn't sure if Randy allowed dogs, but I couldn't very well leave the little guy in my car. Even with the windows cracked, it was way too hot. I might be new to this whole pet-owner thing, but I wasn't an idiot.

"I'll be with you in just a minute," he said, taking a handkerchief out of the back pocket of his overalls and blowing his nose. It sounded like an elephant with a cold—loud and wet. Captain Jack tried to bury his muzzle in my armpit. I felt the same way, but resisted the urge to plug my ears. Randy tucked the handkerchief back into his pocket.

I tried not to stare, but I couldn't see how this man had been married to Paulette. I couldn't imagine her washing his overalls or his handkerchiefs. I was betting all her clothes had been dry-clean-only. He and Paulette must've been like oil and water. As in, motor oil and sparkling mineral water. That's probably why they were divorced.

"Now, what can I do for you?" He looked up for a just a moment, but continued to work.

"My name's Ziva Diaz. I'm a friend of Mrs. Birdie Jackson's."

CLANG. Randy dropped a screwdriver and whatever part he had been holding. I flinched. Captain Jack barked. That was the wrong name to drop.

"What do you want?" He looked up and stared me down while saying the words. I might have been intimidated if he didn't look like he was about to cry.

"Wait, hang on." I held up a hand. "You loved Paulette, am I right?" Of course, I was right. His palms were face down on the counter now, and I could see the indent from the wedding ring he still wore. "Well, I'm here for her because, right now, justice isn't being served and it needs to be."

"Says who?"

"Me. I know Mrs. J.'s not the killer." At least, I was pretty sure she wasn't.

"What's that have to do with me?" Randy looked wary.

"I was hoping you could help me out here, try and figure out who would want to kill Paulette, and don't say Mrs. J..."

Randy closed his eyes and shook his head. "I just don't know what to think. Paulette could be difficult, but not enough to be murdered. She didn't deserve this."

"No enemies?"

"Well now, we hadn't been close for the last couple years, but none that I can think of unless this has something to do with that boyfriend of hers."

"You think Mayor Potts is somehow involved?"

"Wouldn't surprise me. He's a bit of an idiot. Who knows what he could've gotten them into."

I nodded. I could see that. Mayor Potts was the type of

guy who could walk into an armed robbery and not realize it. More than that, I wondered if someone like Whip had it out for him. "I know Mrs. J. and she didn't get along, but did she have a habit of feuding with anyone else?"

"No, no feuding, but you know who I was just thinking about?"

"Who?"

"That Vicki Kline woman. I couldn't remember her name when the police asked me."

"What about her?"

"She was always following Paulette around. An odd duck, that one. Something's off about her."

"Okay, thanks. I'll keep her in mind." Captain Jack wiggled in my arms and I was afraid he might tinkle if I put him down. I gave Randy my card and told him to give me a call if he thought of anything else, and we got out of there. Sitting in my truck, I thought about our next move. What had we learned? One: Randy was still in love with Paulette. Unless it was one of those *"if I can't have her no one else can"* deals, then he wasn't the killer. Two: he was the second person to mention Vicki Kline as a person of interest. Then I remembered what Maryanne said at the hospital about grayantoxins. Plants. *Could it really be all that simple?* Vicki did love her plants. She told me so, but if there ever was anyone who looked less like a murderer, it was her. Then again, what did I know? Last time I tried solving a murder, I became friends with the killer. I definitely couldn't read people as well as I thought I could.

If I turned left, I'd head back toward town. If I turned right, I'd head further toward the country, but maybe that's exactly where I needed to go. If anyone knew about Vicki, it was Suzanne. They clearly weren't friends. Maybe she could tell me why. Plus, I needed to ask Suzanne about purchasing her honey for my products.

Suzy-Bee Honey Farms was about as picturesque as it could be. A small produce stand was at the end of a long, winding driveway stocked with honey jars, fresh-cut flowers, and fresh peaches. Flowering fruit trees lined her driveway, which lead up to a gorgeous white farmhouse with a sweeping front porch and double-door entryway.

Chickens roamed around the front yard and a dog barked somewhere on the property. It all felt very Martha Stewart-ish to me. Captain Jack wanted to get out of my arms, but I had no idea how trained the pup was. Just my luck, he'd bolt for the woods that surrounded the place, and I'd never see him again.

No one answered her door when I knocked, but her white Lexus SUV was parked next to the house, along with a delivery van with the Suzy-Bee logo on it. I wasn't going to snoop, but seeing that I had driven all the way out here, I might as well take a quick peek around the property to see if I could find her.

I walked around the back of the house and was amazed at how beautiful Suzanne's gardens were. The back of the property was even more gorgeous than the front. Blooms in white and purple, and hot pink and yellow dominated the landscape. Everywhere I looked, there were bushes and shrubs, climbing vines, and planter boxes bursting with color. My nose tickled and I knew I'd have to keep my visit short or my allergies would kick into overdrive. Flowers were not my friends. Never had been.

I stopped short at the sight of row upon row of white

beehive boxes arranged in the bright, open yard. Guess I underestimated how many bees it took to make honey. The thought of hundreds or even thousands of bees all buzzing around freaked me out. *Maybe this wasn't the best plan?* I didn't want to be stung. It had been a couple years, but the last time one got me, my hand swelled up to an unhealthy size and I had to chug a bottle of Benadryl. I had pretty much avoided the little winged devils since then. I could never understand how something so cute could inflict so much pain.

Before I could turn tail, I spotted Suzanne a couple rows ahead, working on one of her hive boxes. She appeared to be moving it. I was surprised that she didn't have any protective gear on. Just a straw sun hat, white capris, and a pink button-up blouse. Me? I'd be suited up like I was working with nuclear waste.

Suzanne looked up, startled.

"Hi, sorry, didn't mean to sneak up on you."

"No, that's okay. Just wasn't expecting anyone, that's all." Suzanne had just finished moving one of the hive boxes onto a dolly and was looking inside it, examining it.

"Isn't that dangerous?" I motioned to what she was doing. Captain Jack sniffed toward the box. "Don't put your nose in there, buddy."

Suzanne looked over at Captain Jack but didn't even acknowledge him. Instead, she picked up the smoker at her feet. "It can be, which is why I have this."

I knew bee keepers used them, but I didn't know how one worked. "Does that stun them?"

"Not at all. It actually makes them think there's a fire. When a bee detects smoke, it focuses on consuming honey and protecting the queen, and not so much on what I'm doing." Suzanne took out a piece of broken honey comb. It looked amazing, except for the bees that were starting to swarm. I backed off a little.

"Doesn't the smoke stress them out?" Suddenly, I felt sorry for the little guys. I mean, they were super important pollinators, weren't they?

"I'd rather have them a little stressed out than dead. If you don't smoke them, chances are they'll be more aggressive and sting you. They sting you, they die. So, stress is by far the better alternative."

Well, when you put it that way... "That makes sense." Still, I kept my distance.

"I don't bother them all that often, only to check on the heath of the colony. This one here I'm just getting ready to move."

I had been right, even if I didn't understand why. "I didn't know you could do that." Suzanne looked at me like I was a bit of an idiot. "Sorry, I don't know anything about keeping bees."

"I guess not. Well, of course, you can. Growers rent bees all the time to help with pollination, or I can move the hive to another location if I'm looking to make a particular honey. Of course, we usually move them at night when it's cooler and they're not flying, but this was a special order."

"Really? That's pretty cool. I would've never thought of that." It wasn't a job I was about to sign up for, but it was still interesting.

"So, how can I help you?" Suzanne put the top on the bee box, and I followed her down the row toward the back of her house.

"I actually had a couple things. One is business related. You know I have my own beauty line, and a lot of my products use honey and wax. I was hoping you could help me out. I'd love to use a local supplier."

"Absolutely. How much are you thinking?"

"A few gallons to start and then maybe a pound or two of wax?"

"No problem. JEFFERY!" Susanne hollered and I jumped back. Captain Jack shivered in my arms. *What the heck?* "Where did he go? I swear, that man. Jeffery!"

"It's okay. I don't need it right now. I can come back." *Just stop yelling.* I looked around to make sure the bees weren't getting agitated.

"JEFFERY!"

"Or I can get it. Just point me in the right direction." I looked around as if I could figure out where it was. Thankfully, Jeffery opened the door to the back porch and peered out. He seemed to smile slightly when he saw that I was there. With his long legs, he reached us in a couple of seconds. He went right to Captain Jack and scratched his ears.

"Hey, little guy." Captain Jack licked at his hand. "He's pink?"

"Don't ask," I said, and laughed.

"Jeffery, grab Ziva a couple jugs of honey and that wax bag from the inventory room," Suzanne ordered, interrupting us. No please, no thank you, just orders.

"I can give you a hand," I offered.

"It's okay, he's got it," Suzanne said.

"Sorry," I mouthed to Jeffery. He shrugged his shoulders as if to say he was used to it, and walked off to fetch the goods.

"Jeffery's your husband?" I asked Suzanne when he was out of earshot.

Suzanne snorted. "Good heavens, no! Why would you think that?"

"I'm sorry, I just assumed. I saw him with you at the

farmers market, and he lives here, right?" *I mean, why else would the guy stick around?* He looked a bit younger than her, but not by that much.

"Jeffery's my stepson. My husband passed away a few years ago, but left the business to the two of us."

"Oh...," I guess that made sense. Jeffery was forced to be here or he had to give up his inheritance. *Nice.*

"Jeffery's just like his father—has brains, but not an ounce of business sense. Forget motivation. He'd have honey pouring out of his hiney if it wasn't for me. Bit sad, really. Now, what else do you need?"

"Well, I talked with Randy Berger today."

"Ha, another winner. Smartest thing Paulette ever did was divorcing him. He was going nowhere fast."

I wasn't sure about that. "I don't know, he seemed like an okay guy. His business seemed to be doing pretty well."

"Being an okay guy and doing pretty well sometimes isn't good enough. Know what I'm saying?"

Nope. I didn't. I was thinking good enough was just great. I was beginning to realize just how hard Suzanne, and probably Paulette, were to please, especially if you were a man. Maybe that's why Mayor Potts wasn't so torn up to see Paulette gone? *Maybe he had a motive after all...*

"What were you visiting that lug for?" Suzanne asked.

"I wanted to know what he thought about Paulette. Check him off the list, you know, due diligence. Anyway, he mentioned Vicki Kline. Thinks there's something off about her."

Suzanne laughed. "Of course, there is. She's a bit nutty, always has been."

"What's the story with you guys? I had heard you were friends of sorts." That was putting it nicely.

"Our mothers were all friends."

As if that explained it all. "And?"

"I've been stuck with her for one reason or another ever since. Never been able to shake her." Suzanne brushed a bee off her shoulder as if it was Vicki.

"Paulette too?"

"Vicki annoyed the bejesus out of her. She couldn't stand her. Pretty sure the feeling was mutual."

"Just how strong was this dislike?"

"If you're thinking Vicki had something to do with Paulette..."

"It's possible, isn't it?"

Suzanne just laughed and laughed and laughed. "Vicki? Oh, that's hilarious. The woman cries whenever a flower dies."

I could believe that, but I could also believe that a lifetime of not fitting in could take its toll. It's always the quiet ones you have to watch out for.

"Besides, what are you poking around for? Heard they arrested Birdie this morning. About time. That crazy kook's turned into a killer. Everyone knows she hated Paulette. There's a special place, you know where, she can just go."

Jeffery met us again with a wood crate full of the honey and wax. "This is awesome. Thank you so much. What do I owe you?" I asked him.

"Consider this a free sample." Suzanne spoke for him. "We can talk price if you decide to use it in your products."

11

I left Suzy-Bee Farm and drove back home. Captain Jack pawed at the window until I rolled it down just a crack. I was all in favor for blasting the air conditioning, but the puppy wasn't having it. I just didn't want to roll down the window too far and have him fall out. *Do they make puppy car seats?*

Back home, I couldn't shake that there was more to Vicki, regardless of what Suzanne had said. Vicki seemed sweet to me, unless you messed with her plants. Then watch out. I dug in my purse and pulled out the flyer she gave me yesterday. I had never taken a gardening class before, but I could really use one. Just ask my parents. They no longer asked me to water their plants when they went out of town. Instead, they relied on those automatic water bulbs that you stick in the soil. Something they should've invested in long ago.

I read the information on the flyer. As luck would have it, she taught a class tonight at seven PM. Even better, it was on poisonous plants. I wondered just how much Vicki knew about deadly plants ... and how to make poison. Was it an easy thing to do? Maybe tonight I would find out, or better yet, maybe she would slip up and give me a clue. I used my phone to jump online and register for the class, nabbing the last spot. It looked like I wasn't the only curious person in town.

Other than Vicki, who else did I need to consider? Whip McGovern. More and more I had a feeling that Mayor Pott's had something to do with Paulette's murder, whether intentional or not. I needed to rule out Vicki and then look to Mayor Potts and his associates.

I spent the rest of my afternoon thinking about how I was going to arrange a run-in with the mayoral candidate. What was his story? According to his online campaign schedule, he was hosting a fundraising luncheon tomorrow. Tickets were a hundred dollars a pop, and I couldn't justify spending that kind of dough for a luncheon, murder suspect or not. But that didn't mean I couldn't crash it. I was still thinking about the best way to pull it off when Aria called.

She didn't even wait for me to say hello. "This wedding is a disaster."

"Oh no, what now?" I closed my laptop and stood up to stretch.

"Where in the heck do I even start? You know my dress?" Rhetorical question. "It's gone. I went to pick it up today and they can't even find it. Poof! Just like that. It was there on Friday when I went by."

"How do you lose someone's wedding dress?" I wasn't a fan of the dress, but I still didn't want it to go missing. Talk about a stressful situation.

"I know, right? I have no idea."

"What's your game plan? Do they have another one there, or can they get you one?"

"It's a custom gown!"

"I know, but dude, Vince knows everyone. If anyone can make it happen, he can."

"I know, but he's so stressed out with the kids and work, I don't even want to tell him. He's not even back in town yet. Christina wants me to go dress shopping back home with her to Atlanta, but I don't know. Part of me wants to hold out and see if the shop finds my dress, but I don't want to wait too long."

ARIA'S FAMILY lives in Atlanta and they did have some amazing bridal salons there, but I could see wanting to hold out. "Girl, I'm sorry. That sucks."

"I'm breaking out in even more hives just thinking about it!"

"Okay, just take a breath. You're not driving, are you?"

"I pulled over before I called."

"Okay, good." I didn't need my bestie crashing.

"That's not the worst of it though."

"There's more?" I couldn't even imagine.

"Oh yeah. I called the florist, and they don't have any record of my wedding order. Nothing. They told me to stop in and see what they could do, but there's no guarantee they'll be able to get the flowers I wanted." Aria was like me; she didn't really like flowers. But I'm pretty sure that was a moot point. "I'm headed over there now, and was wondering if you wanted to meet me? Prevent me from throttling someone." You knew Aria was hot if she was looking at me to be the calm, rational one. I mean, she was a yoga instructor. She was paid to spend her days all Zen-like.

I looked at the clock; it was two PM. I could do that, but I wanted to stop by the pet store first and buy a crate for Captain Jack. I couldn't keep taking him everywhere with me, and I needed to make sure he stayed out of trouble. I told Aria to give me thirty minutes and I would meet her at the shop. Fortunately for me, it was just down the street from my apartment. Playing detective was going to have to take a time out. Right now, my girl needed me.

OH, sweet sugar. Aria needed to hurry up and get this wedding business over with before she aged herself over the hill. I wasn't sure my beauty products would be enough to give her that wedding day glow as it was. I've had dark circles before, but my oh my, Aria was rocking the raccoon look, and it wasn't pretty.

"Are you sleeping?" I asked by way of greeting.

"Ha," is all she offered, an un-humorous laugh.

"I don't know, maybe you should go see a doctor, or maybe an acupuncturist or a day spa or something." *Anything.*

"I wouldn't say no to any of those."

I made a mental note to stop by our favorite spa and pick her up a gift certificate.

The flower shop was hopping. It turned out, the mayor had a ton of friends and everyone wanted to send him flowers. The place was crazy. I was betting it wasn't even this busy on Valentine's Day. Unfortunately, the store only had two ladies working, who I knew happened to also be the owners. Betsy and Claire were super sweet ladies, and entirely in over their heads. The elderly sisters had owned Lovely Blossoms since inheriting the shop from their aunt decades ago. Rumor had it that Claire was ready to retire, but Betsy wouldn't hear of it. In fact, she refused to hear much of anything as she never wore her hearing aids.

We tried to wait patiently at the bridal table while the ladies waited on their customers. Betsy rang up sales while Claire customized the order.

"Would you like another rose? Yellow or pink?" she asked the gentlemen at the front of the line. I could appreciate Claire's attention to detail, but man, she was killing me here.

"How about a daisy? Now, one or two?"

I popped an antihistamine.

"What about a card? Did you fill out a card yet? We have a lovely selection," she said to another man, leading him over to the card display.

Noooooo! I looked over at Aria. She was totally zoned out. I let her take a mental vacation. She needed it. In fact, I thought about joining her.

"Sorry about that, girls," Claire addressed us ... ten minutes later. "Now, where is that binder? Betsy, have you seen it?"

"Seen what?" Betsy asked.

"The bridal binder."

"The what?"

"The binder. You know, where we write down our wedding orders?" Betsy still had no idea what Claire was talking about.

"You don't by chance take computer orders, do you?" I asked Claire.

"Oh no, we don't have anything fancy like that. Excuse me for one minute, girls." Claire went back behind the counter and began to rummage through various bins and boxes.

I whispered to Aria, "Who did you place your order with?" She pointed to Betsy. I had a feeling that explained it all.

"Did they give you a written receipt? Anything?"

"No, I didn't think to get one. I placed the order with Betsy and she just asked me to stop in a few days before to pay."

Claire rejoined us with her binder in hand. I could relate. Up until a couple months ago, I lugged all my clients' info around in a similar binder, AKA my *Beauty Bible*. I've since digitized the whole thing and all my orders are online. It made my life easier. Although, I never lost a client's order like Claire here. I saw that the store's orders were paper punched and clipped into the three-ring binder. One could easily slip out. I looked under the table to be sure Aria's wasn't sitting right under our nose. It wasn't.

"Sorry, girls. Now what's the problem again?" Claire had a blank order form in front of her and a pen at the ready.

"My wedding flowers. We're trying to find the order. Everything was red: the roses, lilies, peonies, and I had floating orchids at each place setting."

Claire started writing everything down. "Now when is your wedding, dear?"

"Friday."

"This Friday?" Claire looked incredulous.

"Yes, this Friday," Aria stated as a matter of fact.

"Oh honey, I don't think that's possible. That's a custom order. You needed to make that in advance."

"Yes, you really should've made an advanced order," Betsy had joined us.

I was thinking they both might want to back up. Aria's head might just explode. I put my hand on her arm. "Not worth it." Aria would disagree, but she relented. Not before giving the women a look to end all looks, however.

I took the lead. "Is there any way you could tell us what you could get in?" I asked Claire.

"How about some daisies? They really are the friendliest flower, or what about carnations? I just love carnations. Don't you?" Betsy bobbed her head up and down like Claire had the perfect solution.

Aria dropped her head into her hands.

No, just no. We weren't going to get far here.

12

*A*fter leaving Aria and promising her we could order some awesome wedding flowers online, I decided I needed a little pick-me-up, especially if I was going to attend Vicki's class in a couple hours. That meant a stop in at Sweet Thangs. The bakery was my happy place. Not only did they make the best chai latte ever (seriously, it came with crystalized cinnamon sprinkled on top), but the pastries were heavenly.

I tried to get Aria to come with me, but she was focused on clean eating. I still wasn't sure what that meant, but if chocolate wasn't allowed, then it wasn't for me. *Wait, is chocolate allowed?*

I walked into Sweet Thangs and did a double take. Sitting at a back table, laughing like besties, were Justine and Detective Roxy. I'd like to think Detective Roxy was asking Justine about my sabotaged product launch, but I had a feeling their little get together was more of a social visit. I smiled at Detective Roxy and she looked away. *Yep, Justine definitely told her a thing or two about me.* Only part of it, if that, would be true. Did I mention that I hated Justine?

She was my Paulette, and then I thought the worst. *What if someone murdered Justine?* Horrible to think about, but honestly if it happened, and given our history, I know I'd be a prime suspect. I could only hope nothing suspicious would come of her, even if I'd like to imagine her disappearing every now and then. Meaning move to Hawaii, I swear.

I got a chocolate-filled croissant and chai latte and was going to walk out the door when I changed my mind and walked over to them instead. Younger Ziva would've ignored them, scarfed down her croissant, and cried over how mean girls could be. Mature Ziva didn't tolerate people talking crap about her, especially when I doubted any of it was true. Besides, I was still convinced Justine messed with my products somehow. She would always be guilty until proven otherwise, in my book. I would just have to be careful not to threaten her in front of Detective Roxy.

"Did she ever tell you about the time she keyed Aria's car?" I asked the detective, interrupting their conversation.

"How about the time she banged my boyfriend?" Justine retorted.

"Ex-boyfriend. And you're going to have to be more specific. At the rate you go through men, that pretty much includes all eligible bachelors in a fifty-mile radius." I could've kept going, but I stopped when I took in Justine's wardrobe choice. She was wearing a long-sleeved, high-necked blouse. It was ninety-some degrees outside with the humidity level set to sweat, and Justine was the type who liked to show off all her assets, even if they were silicone-filled. I don't think she even owned a bathing suit cover up. Today's wardrobe choice was so unlike her that it begged me to question what she was hiding, but before I could, Detective Roxy broke up their little tête-à-tête.

"Well, I hate to end this lovely conversation, but I need to get back to work. Justine, it was nice chatting with you. Thanks for all the ...um ... information."

"Oh, I'm sure she was full of all sorts of helpful information," I said.

"Anytime," Justine replied. We did the stare-down-each-other thing that we had perfected over the last twenty years.

Detective Roxy snapped me out of it. "Ziva, you have a minute? I want to chat with you."

I squinted my eyes at Justine for added measure. She stuck out her tongue. I thought about smacking her across the face, but that probably wasn't the smartest thing to do in front of a cop.

Detective Roxy and I stepped outside and walked a few steps down the street.

"We got a match on your lotion. Urushiol," she said.

"Come again?" What was it with all this toxic talk lately? I needed a chemistry degree just to make sense of it all.

"Poison ivy, well the compound that causes you to itch, anyway. Remember I told you it was like I had poison ivy? Well, I had them look for it, and we got lucky."

"No flipping way." I was about to turn on my heel and march back into Sweet Thangs. Detective Roxy as a witness or not, I was going to pummel Justine. I swore on all things holy that I would get back at her.

"Don't, she's already left." Detective Roxy seemed to be a mind reader. Or maybe I was just that transparent.

"Can't you arrest her? Take her in for questioning? Something? Anything so I don't have to just sit around and wait for her to do something else." Because honestly, I wasn't about to sit around much longer and do nothing. I was already planning how to take matters in my own hands, and well, not go to jail for it.

"We need to have some evidence or an eye witness, something more than just your hunch."

"Years of disdain doesn't count?"

"Not when arresting someone. I tried talking to her, but she didn't offer up much. Do you have anything else?"

"Not yet," I said with a mischievous smile.

"I did not hear that, but let me know what you find out."

"Don't worry, I will."

RUNNING into Justine reminded me that I needed to rebrand my business. Bye-bye, Serenity Now. I didn't even want to try and salvage that company's reputation. I needed to come up with a new name, which I was more than okay with as Serenity Now had been Mrs. DeVine's idea. I went back through my original ideas. I wanted to incorporate a part of me into my business's name, but still allow people to know what the business was all about. Hence why Chocolate Lover was out. I ended up writing up a list of all the adjectives that described me (smart, sassy, sophisticated. Okay, maybe not that last one), and things that I loved (chocolate, cake, sugar, and shoes) to come up with Sugar & Sass Skincare. Now I just needed to contact my designer and get her to mock up a new logo, and I needed to file for a new LLC license and DBA papers, and update my website. It was going to be a heck of a lot of extra work, but worth it. I thought once I had all the branding in place and market research to back it up, Mrs. DeVine would be totally cool with the change. At least, I hoped she would.

That night at 6:45 PM, after spending all afternoon working on the rebrand, I parked in front of the conservatory and headed inside. The conservatory was housed in a large, glass dome building with open-aired gardens and smaller glass houses connected to it. The architecture was impressive, the flowers gorgeous, and my allergies in check, thanks to the mountain of antihistamines I loaded up on before class. Good thing they were the non-drowsy kind.

I had no idea what to expect. The course description didn't mention anything about supplies, but like a good student, I brought a notebook and pen along. I wondered if I should've brought gardening gloves. I was not touching anything.

I walked down the hall, past the auditorium, and into a small classroom on the right. Several potted plants some with vines, or covered in tiny hairs, and others with beautiful blooms were displayed on a metal table at the front of the room. Next to each one was a sign that said DON'T TOUCH and POISONOUS with the skull and crossbones image above it. Just looking at the plants, I would have never guessed they were poisonous. Thirty people or so were already in the room. The way they chitchatted told me that they all mostly knew one another. A woman named Inez walked in after me. Inez was one of my beauty clients who loved to talk as much as she loved her flowers. She had been born with the gift to gab, as my nan used to say. She was also Vince's grandmother, although she called him Tico. I had no idea they were related until I saw him over at her house one day, but that's another story.

"Well, hello, Ziva. I wasn't expecting to see you here today. Such a wonderful surprise!" Inez took a seat next to me. "I had no idea you were into gardening. You never said anything before. Now we have something else to talk about. Oh, and aren't you excited for this weekend? I found the perfect dress. Tico took me shopping at Nordstrom!"

Now that was something I could talk about. I loved

Nordstrom's shoe department. Once I got this mess straight-ened out, I was rewarding myself with a new pair of heels. I saw the cutest pair of gold strappy sandals there a couple weeks ago that I haven't been able to get out of my mind. I was starting to feel even more motivated to find out who killed Paulette and poisoned the mayor. Shoes motivated me like that.

"Did you hear that the mayor was poisoned?! I bet that's what all these people are here for." Inez looked around the room. "I wonder if Vicki's working on the case?" Now that was something I hadn't thought of. I should've given her name to Detective Roxy this afternoon along with her and Paulette's history. If all checked out, Detective Roxy would probably appreciate someone like Vicki on her team.

Vicki walked in then, wearing safety glasses and heavy-duty gardening gloves up to her elbows. This looked serious. *Maybe I shouldn't have picked a spot in the front row?*

Vicki welcomed us all and started the class by asking us if we could identify any of the plants before her. Inez's hand shot up and startled me. Someone was going to be an *A* student, and it wasn't going to be me.

"Well, first you have Water Hemlock. Looks lovely like Queen Anne's lace, but it'll kill you in a heartbeat. That's a wicked little plant. Next to that, you have the nefarious stinging nettle. Don't get too close to that one! On the end, there is the castor bean plant. They say the seeds are more poisonous than rattle snack venom!"

"Ah yes, ricinus communis. Everything on this one is poisonous. It's big and the color is bold, but it's also deadly. One bean and—" Vicki pretending to cut her throat with her finger. "Lights out."

I scooted my chair back an inch.

Vicki continued, "The saying goes: the difference is in

the dosage. Some poisonous plants become powerful medicines when taken at the appropriate dosage. Take foxglove and digitalis. The blooms make for beautifully cut flowers, and butterflies love them," Vicki walked over to a vase filled with yellow and peachy bell-shaped flowers, "but the plant itself is toxic. People have died by confusing it with the comfrey plant, which herbalists use to make tea. Pets have also been poisoned by drinking the water in a vase containing the flowers."

I thought of poor Captain Jack at home. *What type of flowers are in the vase on my kitchen table? Are they harmful to him? And what other dangers are lurking around my apartment?* Looks like I had some serious puppy proofing to do, and soon. Good thing he was in his crate right now.

"But digitalis extracted from the plant is used to treat a variety of heart conditions. You'll find the same thing with belladonna," Vicki continued.

"Deadly nightshade," Inez chimed in.

"Right. It's extremely toxic, especially the berries, but it could also save your life. You can thank the plant's component of atropine for that. If you're in cardiac arrest or have pesticide poisoning, you'll be very grateful for this one." Vicki was in her element. This was the most animated I had ever seen her.

"And what about this one?" Vicki brought a small potted plant forward on the table. It had clusters of lovely green leaves and looked totally harmless to me. This time, several hands shot up in the air.

Inez whispered to me, "Well, everyone knows that's poison ivy." I nodded my head as if I couldn't agree more. The clueless gardener, that's me.

"I'm sure you've all heard the adage, *Rules of three, let it be*, or *Hairy vine, no friend of mine.* But did you also know it can grow as a shrub?" Vicki held up a picture of an impressive-looking bush. With it's beautiful yellow flowers and lush leaves, I never would've thought it was the same plant as the vine in front of me.

"Here are a couple other fun facts for you. The urushiol compound in the plant, which is responsible for our misery, is actually what helps the plant retain water. Several animals take advantage of this, like deer and bears. They can snack on the plant with no problem. The plant is a member of the cashew and almond family. A similar compound to urushiol is found in the raw shells of cashews."

Hmmm, well, scratch cashews off my shopping list.

I thought of a question to ask and raised my hand. "So, with poison ivy, is there a way to squeeze the juice out of it or something?" I was trying to figure out how Justine would've gotten the compound into my products.

Vicki looked at me strangely and was probably wanting to know why I wanted to know, but she answered my question anyway, "You could. It's the sap that's in the plant where the urushiol is contained. I suppose you could milk it, so to speak."

"Oh, good to know. I was just, um ... curious." *Wow, that lie was awful.* Inez gave me the side eye. "I'll tell you later," I told her.

A couple other people asked a few questions, which Vicki easily answered, and then she continued to show us poisonous plants that were native to the area. I seriously had no idea there were so many plants that could kill you, and many of them in your own backyard.

Vicki asked if anyone else had any other questions and I took a chance. "What about grayanotoxins?" I hoped I pronounced it correctly.

Vicki studied me for a minute. "What about them?"

"What is it from? Is it common to the area?" I wanted to know how easy it had been for the killer to get his or her hands on the poison.

"Very much so. The toxin is derived from azaleas, also known as the Georgia State Wildflower."

You gotta be kidding me. Azaleas I knew. The flowering shrubs were everywhere and they made me sneeze something fierce every single spring. How was Detective Roxy supposed to narrow it down when you could literally pick the poison from almost anyone's backyard?

I didn't ask any more questions after that. I thought whoever had chosen azaleas to make poison out of was pretty smart. *Vicki* was pretty smart.

13

The next morning, my first stop was at the groomer. I hoped they had some magical shampoo to wash the pink out of my puppy's fur. This morning when he woke, I noticed some pink dye had rubbed off on my white down comforter. My bedding was an easy fix, but if the stains started showing up on my couch and clothes, then I was going to have a problem. I wasn't sure what could be done for his ridiculous drawn-on eyebrows, but I was up to letting them try. Captain Jack looked at me like I was a traitor when I dropped him off, but I promised him a special treat if he was a good boy. He didn't look happy. He sure wasn't going to like it when I took him to the vet.

Next up was a trip to the pharmacy for my monthly girl-supply run. I found that it was best to always be prepared where your period was concerned. Maybe if I was feeling extra brave this month, I'd try out a pair of those fancy-shmancy period panties. I heard they were quite amazing. But until then, I hit up the candy aisle first. Chocolate bars were buy two, get one free. Who could pass that up? I was after all, a proud member of the twelve-step chocoholic program. You know, never be more than twelve steps from chocolate? Let me tell you, that was a good motto to live by. I added six bars to my basket and kept on shopping. Ice cream was on sale too. Both were necessities in my book. I added two pints to my basket, promising I'd save one for Finn. Maybe.

And then the drama happened.

There I was, perusing the tampons and panty liners when I heard a voice that I would recognize anywhere, even if she was dressed incognito. I peered around the end cap and spotted Justine talking one-on-one with a pharmacist. Her cheese-doodle hair was tucked under a baseball cap, and she was sporting tight jeans and an oversized sweatshirt. This was about as undercover as she'd ever been. Something was definitely up.

I walked down the next aisle to get a better look.

Justine pushed up her sleeve, revealing a nasty, blistering rash on her arm. It was the same one my other clients had been sporting, only hers looked much worse. I had two conflicting thoughts in that instant. One: Justine must've gotten some of the poison ivy sap on her when she was tampering with my products; or two: Justine had been using my products and thus was another victim. I liked imagining her as the perpetrator versus the victim, by far. Either way, it explained why she didn't want to be seen. She'd either be admitting her guilt or that she'd been using my products. I stood there wondering what I should do. *Do I want Justine to see me, or do I want to let her think I'm still in the dark?*

My reflexes made up my mind for me.

Justine turned from the pharmacist and headed my way. I whipped around so fast that I crashed right into the family planning end cap. Pregnancy tests, condoms, and personal lubricants toppled onto the floor. One of the bottles rolled under my heel, tripping me up and sending me falling onto my butt. I sat dumbfounded on the tiled floor for a second, looking at the mess around me. *Whoops.*

Miraculously, Justine didn't see me. My bet was she was eager to get out of there and didn't want to be seen any more than I wanted her seeing me. I stood up and rubbed my back end, apologizing to the sales associate who ran over to help me. I looked around, but Justine was already gone. *What is she up to now?*

I COULDN'T SPEND all morning thinking about Justine. Not when I had a murder to solve, and a realtor to meet up with. Today was the day that I was set to sign lease papers on my new storefront. Part of me felt guilty, as I hadn't fessed up to Mrs. DeVine about what happened at the farmers market, and she was my financial backer. The other part thought that I had everything under control and once I had Justine on the hook, I'd have her make a public apology and that would be the end of that. I might not be able to win those customers back, but hopefully I could stop the bad press and potential lawsuits.

I pulled in front of the vacant storefront. It was wedged between a day spa and a shoe store. I couldn't have asked for a better location, well unless a spot next to Sweet Thangs opened up. But in terms of product placement, this was the best. I was hoping to naturally pick off some of my neighbors' clients. I had already thought of offering a ten-percent discount to either of their customers if they showed me a recent receipt. I peered inside at the wide-planked pine floors and white shelves just waiting to be stocked. The only major addition it needed was a washing station on the side somewhere. A place where people could try out my exfoliators and soaps. I could picture it in my mind, a white porcelain farmhouse sink with a brushed nickel faucet. I was hoping Finn would give me a hand with the plumbing part. He was, after all, good with his hands. My phone buzzed in my pocket and snapped my mind out of the gutter. I was hoping it was my realtor, Cassandra, saying she was on her way. Seeing the time made me realize she was already ten minutes late.

But it wasn't. It was Aria. I was starting to dread her calls. How awful was that?

"What's up, love?" I asked.

"It's gotten worse."

"I was afraid of that. What's going on?"

"I had Christina check in with the caterer, because I'm paranoid like that now, and turns out the last party they did, a bunch of people got sick."

"Sick? Like how?"

"Food poisoning."

"Oh gross." Throwing up rated right up there with watching people cry. *Then again, maybe I'd rather throw up.*

"So, now I'm stuck. I'm not sure if I want to just chance it or if I should rush out and try to book someone else."

"What did Vince say? Oh wait, never mind. But you should seriously probably clue him in to what's going on. I'm sure he'd want to know."

"I know. He comes home tonight. I'd love to have this all straightened out beforehand though."

"I hear ya." After all, I wanted to do the same thing with Mrs. DeVine and my business drama.

"So, what do you want to do now?"

"I guess I'm going to keep the caterer on the line and

make a few calls. See if there's anyone else even willing to take on a wedding with this short notice. What are you doing?"

"Supposed to meet my realtor, but she's not here yet. Let me give her a call and see what's up. I'll call you back. Maybe we could meet for brunch?" I was thinking we could both use a mimosa right now. *Maybe two.*

I hung up with Aria and tried to reach Cassandra. No luck. I left her a message telling her where I was and reminded her that I was ready to sign the lease. Hopefully, she'd call me back in a hot second and we could meet up to the sign the papers, but five minutes went by without even a text. I took it a step further and sent her an email pretty much saying the same thing and then called back Aria and told her I'd meet her in ten.

I WAS SIPPING my mimosa on the outside patio of Le Crêpes Café when Cassandra called back. Our waiter had just delivered our crepes—strawberry, chocolate, and cream cheese for me; spinach and feta for Aria—but I left it untouched, eager for some good news.

"Hey girl, thanks for getting back with me. I thought we were supposed to meet up this morning?" I said.

"And I thought you didn't want the property anymore. Something about your products being contaminated?" Cassandra sounded unsure.

"What? Said who?" I hadn't spoken to Cassandra since my birthday. I knew news travelled fast in a small town, but not fast enough for a realtor to back out of a commission.

"Said you, in your email, Sunday night."

"I never emailed you."

"Well, that's weird."

I had another word for it, but instead I said, "You have no idea. Listen though, I still want to rent the space. Is it available?"

"I'm not sure. I know there were a couple other interested parties. Let me pull it up and see where it's at and give you a call back."

Ugh. Great. "Okay, thanks. Let me know as soon as possible. I want to get it on lockdown." I hung up with Cassandra and stared at my crepe, not even hungry anymore.

"What was that all about?" Aria asked.

"Girl, let me tell you, that's my life right now. You know how your wedding is going to hell? Well, so's my business." I filled Aria in on my missing shipment and what the realtor had just said.

"It's definitely like someone's messing with us," I said.

"But who?"

"You know who I'm going to say."

"Justine."

"Of course."

"But, why would she mess with me? And my wedding? She usually just tries to make only your life miserable."

"I know, right? I don't know. Maybe she's kicked her craziness up to a new level?"

"You mean since her ex is your new boyfriend?"

"He's not my boyfriend."

"Oh, come on! Get over yourself and your weird aversion to titles. How many days do you go without talking to him?"

Well, let's see. He's been out to sea since Saturday, so, "three."

"When he's not working?"

My silence told her all she needed to know. Truthfully, Finn and I talked or texted several times a day. More than I talked to Aria lately.

"And I know you're with him all the time. Trust me, Christina's already reminded me a million times how much more she's helped me with this wedding than you."

I started to protest.

"Not that you're not busy. Trust me, I get it. I'm not worried about us, just quit trying to dismiss your relationship with Finn. He's a good guy. Don't scare him away with your issues. He's not Todd."

"I know. Todd was a jerk." Todd: my ex-fiancé who cheated on me with at least one other girl and then tried to blame me for it.

"He was much worse than a jerk."

"I was being polite."

"I like Finn. You like Finn. Don't screw it up."

"Thanks, Mom."

Aria flipped me off. See? We were just like sisters.

I changed the subject, even though Aria's words stuck with me. She was right. I knew that. I just didn't need her to know that, not yet. I was just coming around to the idea myself.

"Speaking of Todd..." Aria trailed off.

I cringed at his name. "I'm not sure I even want to know."

"No, what I was going to say was, do you think it's possible he's the one messing with you?"

"Why would you think that?"

"Um, because you keyed his car and it was a Porsche?"

I smiled at the fond memory. "Okay, that may be true, but he had good insurance, so it's not like he had to pay for it. I mean, besides his deductible."

"I highly doubt it's the money aspect of it that ticked him off."

Aria might have a point. He did love that car. "Well, he totally deserved it."

"I agree, but who knows, maybe he's been quietly waiting to get his revenge."

Ugh. Aria was on a roll today. I blew out a big puff of air while I thought about it. "I don't even know where he is."

"Ah! But I do."

"Of course, you do." Aria signaled for another round of drinks. I was thinking I should switch to vodka, considering where this conversation was headed.

14

It turned out Todd was working on Whip's campaign, which I guess shouldn't have surprised me, since they both looked full of themselves. Todd had appeared with Whip at Vince's most recent who's-who shindig, and Aria got the scoop from her husband-to-be. "Keep your friends close, your enemies even closer," she reminded me. I knew that was true, but I didn't want to be anywhere near Todd.

As Aria was Vincent Delgado's fiancée, we were more than welcome to attend the campaign luncheon. Well, she was. I was still crashing. I was sure Todd would have me out on my derriere if he spotted me. I had planned on posing as the wait staff, but this change in plans required a serious wardrobe change. Aria's closet was probably the best place to shop anywhere. You know those closets in the movies with a ridiculous number of mirrors, shoes, jewelry and dresses? Yeah, that was Aria's closet.

I chose a nude-colored, form-fitting satin dress. It hugged my curves and gave the girls just a little extra oomph. Nothing too ridiculous or revealing. Not going for

Kim Kardashian here. Just enough to remind Todd of what he lost, you know, in case I ran into him. Putting the dress on reminded me of the shoes I was going to buy as soon as I solved this case. They would've looked awesome with this dress. As it was, I had to settle for a pair of nude-colored pointed heels with only a two-inch heel. I shrugged. It worked, but the gold sandals would've looked better.

We took Aria's little red sports car to Ivy's, where the luncheon was being held. This type of event required a classier ride than my pickup. I was done asking Aria when she was going to sell her late husband's ride. Just as she was done pretending that she didn't love it.

"I've never been to one of these things. What do we do?" I asked Aria. As she was marrying into money again, I was confident she had campaign luncheons on lockdown.

Aria waved her hand to dismiss my concerns. "You know, smile, chit chat, pretend that you care what the candidate has to say."

"Got it. So pretty much like Vince's shindigs and Mrs. DeVine's gatherings, minus the business opportunities."

"Exactly."

We pulled in front of Ivy's and got out to have the car valeted. Several other people dressed to the nines were already in front of us. Aria immediately spotted someone she knew, and the questions about the wedding flowed. Aria smiled and talked about how excited she was. Only I noticed that she started to scratch her upper arm and tug on her dress. I had a feeling her mind was wandering to the current mess her nuptials were in. We'd have to tackle that next.

We quickly realized that the entire restaurant had been reserved for this afternoon's events. Port Haven was a small town, but it had quite a few residents with money, and they appeared to all be present. *Maybe this will be a business opportunity after all.* Aria left to get us a cocktail and I started working the room. Out of the corner of my eye, I spotted the same reporter slash detective guy from earlier in the week. The man was wearing the same tan trench coat and fedora, doing a poor job of hiding out behind a fake tree. He raised his phone and snapped a couple pictures before darting back out the door. *What in the world?*

I dropped that thought when goosebumps surfaced on my skin. I looked around to find out what was giving me the creepy crawlies only to see Whip eyeing me up. He licked his lips and shot me a wining grin, complete with a wink when I made eye contact. I fought the urge to say *oh gross*! Believe me, it wasn't easy. But I wanted to play my cards right. Yes, he totally thought he was all that, but now I had an invitation to go over and introduce myself. He didn't give me a chance.

With his chest puffed and his long stride, Whip was at my side in less than a minute. "Why hello," he said, taking my hand. I meant to give him handshake. He raised it to his lips instead. "Let me introduce myself. Whip. Whip McGovern. But you already knew that, didn't you?" he said with a boisterous laugh.

Oh brother. I pulled my hand away, not letting it linger, and nonchalantly wiped it on the back of my dress.

"I always enjoy meeting a beautiful face, wouldn't you agree?" Whip turned to the side so I could see his profile. Sure, he had a strong nose and square jawline, but I could see there wasn't much between the eyes.

"Sure, yeah, I like meeting people." It didn't really matter what they looked like though.

"You should come to all my campaign events. Wait until you hear my speech. You'll love it."

I doubted that.

"Back when I was at Yale, I gave an excellent presentation on the economic hardships facing the South."

"I bet that was amazing." Only problem was, he never went to Yale. From what I'd learned, he had only played two seasons of lacrosse at the community college before dropping out.

It looked like Whip didn't know sarcasm when he heard it either. "Oh, believe me, it was. I was a real presidential scholar."

I didn't get a chance to respond. At that moment, my ex stopped over to whisper something in Whip's ear. That's when Todd spotted me.

He stopped dead still. Our eyes locked and the color drained completely from his face. I guess I didn't have to worry about him throwing me out. He was dumbfounded. I smiled, as it was the polite thing to do (my mother would be proud) while he continued to stare like an idiot. I hoped he would take a breath soon. I didn't need him keeling over. Who needed that type of bad karma? The mayor episode had already used up all the good graces I had stored.

Whip didn't catch it as Todd was standing behind him.

Aria rejoined me and raised a glass of champagne at Todd. "Hi Todd, how are you?"

He still didn't speak, and I raised my eyebrows, waiting for him to say something. The words, "Excuse me," tumbled out of his mouth as he turned tail and scurried away.

"Yes, excuse us. I would love to continue our chat and meet..."

"Aria. Aria Delgado." My friend shook the egoist's hand, giving him the same once-over I had.

It was Whip's turn to raise his eyebrows. Delgado's name did that to people.

"Or, it will be by Friday," she added.

"Yes, well then it really is a shame, but I assure you I will look for you ladies when I'm done with this speech business." Whip did look disappointed, which told me that he didn't truly care about Port Haven and being Mayor as much as he cared about himself.

He said goodbye and Aria turned to me. "Are we waiting around?"

"Heck no. Whip is totally ridiculous."

We skedaddled out of there as quickly as possible without seeming like we were running away, and waited until we were back in the car to debrief.

"So, Todd," Aria said and then we both started laughing, because honestly, his reaction was priceless.

"Well, if you weren't on his radar, you are now," she said.

"I know, what do you suppose was up with that?"

"You shocked him, that's for sure."

"He looked scared, right?" I asked.

"Definitely. Like maybe you were going to kick his ass."

I smiled at that. A year and a half ago, that could've been a real possibility. But he had nothing to worry about now. He wasn't worth it. I could see that plain as sugar. Here I was smokin' hot while he looked ... vanilla. *What did I ever see in him?* I sent up a quick prayer to my nan, thanking her again for saving me from marrying him. I could've sworn I heard her say, *"anytime."* I pondered what my nana would've thought about Finn, and I instantly smiled. She would've loved him. I started to sigh but snapped myself out of it. Now wasn't the time to turn into a lovesick teenager. We needed to talk more about Todd and Mr. Ego.

I shivered. "I'm still not sure if Todd was shocked because it's been awhile and here I show up looking like this...," I motioned to myself.

"Hot," Aria supplied.

"Or, if it's because he's the one messing with me and he's scared that I know."

"Girl, I don't know either, but if he is causing all this crap, I bet he's rethinking a few things right about now."

"True, but I'm not letting him get off that easy if he is the culprit."

"So, that still leaves Justine."

"Oh, I didn't tell you about that. I ran into her this morning at the pharmacy. Well, I ran into a shelf, but I saw her, and let me tell you, she is up to something fishy." I filled Aria in on Justine and the rash.

"I say we run a little recon tonight and see what she's up to," Aria offered.

"I was hoping you would say that."

15

I was cutting it close that afternoon. Luckily my replacement shipment was delivered on time and I had the rest of my sample packs ready to roll. This month's promo featured lip gloss and nail polish in vivid colors. My favorites were the Rebel nail polish—a dark, rich blue; and the Sunburst lip gloss—a bright coral color. I snatched one of each for myself and planned on pairing it with a soft pink eye shadow and smidge of light shimmer on my cheeks. In my opinion, that was the only problem with being a Beauty Secrets consultant, you had to look put together all the time.

My dad showed up just as the second coat on my nails was drying. I had asked him to puppy-sit Captain Jack, seeing my pup had spent a stressful morning at the groomer and I didn't want to make him spend the evening in his crate. The groomer completely washed out Jack's fake eyebrows, but after several washes, the captain still had some pink tones in his fur. However, he no longer looked quite as ridiculous. In fact, his color was more in line with recent color trends. My dad readily agreed to watch him, seeing I had cable and a comfy couch. I even offered to pick up some brews for the fridge. This was why I was an awesome daughter.

"I might be a little late," I told my dad, while loading up my truck.

"I thought Finn was out of town?"

"Dad!" He chuckled.

"I like him, just so you know."

I thought about being annoyed at everyone telling me how much they liked my boyfriend lately, but I let it go. Until I realized that I just mentally thought of Finn as my boyfriend and started to freak out a little.

"You okay?" Dad asked.

"Yeah, I'm just used to thinking of all men as scum. Sorry. Present company excluded."

"Todd was scum. I never liked him, and I should've told you that."

"You didn't?" This was news to me. My dad never said a word about the men I dated.

"No, but your mother made me swear to keep my mouth shut. She didn't want to ruin your happiness and thought you were a better judge of who was right for you than I was."

"Mom just wanted to see me married."

"Well, there's that too."

"Okay, make me a deal. If you think I'm dating a jerk, give me a heads up. I don't care what Mom says. She's obviously not going to tell me the truth."

"Got it, but like I said, Finn's a good guy."

"Noted."

"Now, what is it you girls are doing?"

"Um, paying a visit to Justine? Recon mission." I winked.

"Don't get arrested."

"Don't plan to."

"And if you do, call my cell phone, and don't forget to use

the shaving cream. Remember, the foam doesn't stick as well." I may or may not have shaving creamed Justine's house a time or two. Although, I think the best was when I turned her car into a moving pancake; that is, smeared butter, syrup and pancake mix all over it. Hey, it was high school and she totally deserved it.

"Keep an eye out for her here, too. I think she's up to her usual crap. And don't tell Mom!" I turned to walk out the door.

"Hey, Ziva?" I turned back around. "Take the Buick. Justine won't know to look for it." He tossed me his car keys. "Call if you need backup."

"Will do." This, once again, was why my dad was the best.

I ADORED it when Marion hosted Beauty Secrets parties. Not only did she always have a fabulous turnout, but her dessert spread was fantastic. Tonight, she featured buttercream-frosted sugar cookies cut in the shapes of high heels and lipsticks, chocolate-covered strawberries, raspberry crème petit fors, and mini peanut butter chocolate cheesecakes. *Swoon.* This, of course, was in addition to a signature creamsicle cocktail of vanilla vodka, triple sec with a splash of orange juice and half and half. Now that was refreshing. Today was turning out to be one cocktail-infused day, but I wasn't complaining. It was good to have some days like that.

I had done my spiel and working the room, answering questions and promising quick deliveries (as long as they weren't stolen) when a woman in her mid-to-late fifties approached me. She looked regal, with her hair swept up and dangly diamond earrings. I had noticed her eying me throughout the night. I didn't think too much of it as people tended to scrutinize your makeup a little more than usual at these shindigs, but then she said, "I thought you looked familiar, and I just placed it. You were talking to my son today."

Creamsicle cocktail almost shot out of my nose. *That's not what I was expecting.* "Excuse me, sorry, wrong pipe. Your son, you said?"

"Yes, you were at Whip's fundraiser this afternoon, weren't you?"

"That I was."

"I thought so. I loved your dress. Who's the designer?"

"Oh, I'm not sure, but thank you...," *I might have to borrow that one from Aria a little longer so Finn can see me in it.*

"You know, Whip's father would've been so proud of him."

"Oh, was he in politics?"

"It wasn't meant to be," Mrs. McGovern said with wistful eyes. "It was probably for the best as he did just fine as a businessman. But enough with that. I just wanted to say that I saw you two talking today and I thought you made a very fine-looking couple."

Ah, and there it was; she wanted to hook me up with her son. I did the inward cringe thing, but managed to say, "Oh, that's so sweet of you, but I'm actually seeing someone."

"Is it serious?" Mrs. McGovern asked as a matter of fact.

Maybe. Could be. Not sure yet. What was it with people bugging me about my relationship status lately? *Gah!* "Yes, yes it is," I lied. But hey, it could be. "I thought your son was very nice though." *If superficial egos were my cup of tea.*

Mrs. McGovern looked disappointed, but she was going to have to live with it. No way was I dating Whip. Finn or no Finn, that was not happening. I excused myself and went over to check in with Marion to see how she thought the party was going.

I stayed until the last guest left to close out the party and go over Marion's hostess gifts and earned rewards. Like usual, Marion received all the bonuses and was even entered in the Grand Beach Getaway contest. Now that was something I'd like to win, an all-expense paid vacation at the beach, preferably without a dead body.

"So, I think that's it. Tonight went pretty well, didn't it?" I said.

"I think so." Marion was getting ready to put on a pot of tea. She reminded me of my mother in this regard.

"You had some new faces here too. I talked to Mrs. McGovern. She seemed nice..."

"Oh, Caroline? She's something all right. I've known her and her late husband, Bob, for years."

"Oh yeah, she mentioned something about him and politics."

"Did she now?" Marion rolled her eyes and shook her head.

"What? What's that all about. You have to tell me now."

"It's just that Bob was a bit of a schmoozer. Thought of himself as a smooth talker. About the only thing he couldn't talk himself into was office."

"What did he run for?"

"Bob thought he was headed to Washington. Congress, I believe. When that didn't pan out, he set his sights on running Port Haven."

"Ah, like Whip. I get it now."

"Exactly. It was a pretty heated race. You know how nasty politics can be. I don't have to tell you how it ended."

"Who was he running against?"

"Oh, Humphrey Potts, of course. Those two ridiculous

men ended up hating each other until the day Bob died."
Marion shook her head. "And Humphrey's has been our
mayor ever since. Don't think he's had a serious contender
either. Well, not unless you count Whip now."

So, Whip had a family vendetta against Mayor Potts?
Sounded as good as any motive to me.

And maybe he killed off Paulette to dig the knife a little deeper.
I wasn't sure how if all fit together, but I was determined to
figure it out.

I LOOKED at the clock as I pulled out of Marion's driveway
and headed to meet Aria. It seemed much later than eight
thirty.

I nabbed a couple extra mini cheesecakes and chocolate-
covered strawberries for tonight's mission before leaving the
party. That was as healthy of an option Aria was going to get.
Aria met me in the parking lot of the Piggly Wiggly. I texted
her beforehand to be on the lookout for my parents'
Enclave.

"What's the game plan?" Aria said when she got in. She
was dressed in dark-print leggings with a black t-shirt. I
looked down at my bright blue skinny jeans and off-the-
shoulder white shirt. *I did not think this through.*

"Look in the bag," Aria said. I did and noticed she had
thrown in a similar dark-hued outfit for me. This is why she
was my best friend.

I climbed in the back and did a quick wardrobe change.
While I did, I said, "I figured we'd swing by Justine's place
and see if she's in. If not, we'll take a little lookie-loo inside
and see if we spot anything suspicious."

"Like a bunch of poison ivy plants growing on her kitchen table?"

"Exactly. We just need to keep an eye out for Withers."

"Who's that? New dog?"

"Ha, no. Apparently, he's her butler." Aria gave me the look. "I know. Either that, or it's some new fetish. I'm not sure which."

We pulled in front of Justine's house just in time to see a black Porsche pull away. Even without a few choice words etched into the side, I'd recognize that car anywhere. The question was, where were Justine and Todd headed?

We skipped snooping and followed them instead.

Ariana and I hung back, doing our best PI impersonation, and followed the two of them as they merged onto the highway. Traffic was light, but I wasn't worried. It was starting to finally get dark and I was confident neither of them would recognize my dad's car.

They bypassed the strip clubs that cluttered the highway along the way, which honestly was a bit of a surprise. I wouldn't put it past Justine to suggest a stop off until I remembered who she was with; Todd, Mr. Vanilla.

We crossed into Georgia and could see Savannah in the distance. By the time we got off on Oglethorpe Avenue, I had a hunch of where they were headed. When they turned left onto Martin Luther King Jr. Boulevard and we got the light, I wasn't worried.

"Shoot, we're gonna lose them," Aria said.

"No, we won't." We turned left onto West Broughton and right on Montgomery, coming to Congress just in time to see Todd park in front of O Sole Mio. The Italian restaurant had been a favorite of his and was the very spot where he had proposed to me. I shuddered, recalling his horrible speech about not getting any younger, so we might as well... I should've stopped him right there, but man, that ring was blinding.

"Isn't that where..." Aria asked. I nodded. "Oh vomit."

"Right? Glad to see he's trying something new."

"You feel up for some calamari?" Aria asked.

"Not hardly. Let's hang back. I don't want them to see us. But don't worry, I brought dessert."

A LITTLE OVER two hours later, the mini cheesecakes and strawberries had been long since consumed, and Aria snored peacefully next to me, giving me some time to think.

Here was the thing. I wasn't mad at Justine for dating Todd. She could have him. In some sick-twisted way, they were perfect for one another. The problem was, I couldn't help but think this was more than a budding relationship. Throw in their mutual hatred for me, someone sabotaging my business, and Justine's mysterious rash, and it was highly suspect. It couldn't just be a coincidence. Now I needed to think of how to proceed. I know I told Aria that I didn't want them to see us, but a big part of me wanted to confront them, to make a big scene and call them both out on all their crap. The only hitch was, once again, I didn't have any proof.

I took a long calming breath and wished I still had some cheesecake.

It wasn't easy, but eventually I decided I would try to be an adult and attempt to gather some evidence instead of acting like a psycho. Trust me, it was a challenge. I liked to think of it as character growth.

I nudged Aria awake when Justine and Todd walked hand-in-hand out of the restaurant. Under the canopy of the restaurant, while a soft rain started to fall, Todd reached his hand up behind Justine's cheese-doodle hair and went in for a kiss.

"Oh gross, you woke me up for this?"

I felt the same way.

$\mathcal{A}$ria called me first thing Wednesday morning. It was early, too early, but I would forgive her. The bridal salon still hadn't found her dress and she was in panic mode. T-minus three days until her nuptials, and she needed a dress.

"I know you're super busy, but I have a huge favor. Can you come to Atlanta with me today?" she asked.

No, no I cannot. I could not afford to lose a day right now, not with the rebranding of Sugar & Sass and trying to solve a crime; I had plenty that needed my attention in Port Haven. I got a small headache just thinking about it all.

I could hear Christina in the background, "Told you she was too busy. Why did you even call her? We don't need her to come with us."

Christina's bratty attitude had me doing a one-eighty. "What time are we leaving?"

~

SUPER BIG SHOUT out to Vince's grandma, Inez, for watching

Captain Jack, and on such short notice. All Aria had to tell her was that it was a dress emergency and she was more than happy to watch the little guy, even if it was potentially overnight. It was an eight-hour roundtrip to Atlanta and back. I had a feeling it was going to be a very long day. Especially when I climbed into the backseat of Christina's Lexus and saw an itinerary laid out for me. We had a twelve o'clock appointment at the bridal salon, followed by manicures and pedicures at Posh, and dinner reservations at "The Club," which I assumed was Christina's family's country club. Christina eyed my outfit. I had worn a pair of leggings with a flowy shirt, ballet flats, and oversized shades, going for comfort with a little style. Christina was dressed head to toe in white, with a white summer suit and heels. She had even woven a white ribbon into a braid that circled her head like a tiara. Personally, I thought she looked tacky. If anyone should be decked out in white it was the bride-to-be, not that Aria would ever dress like that. Like I said, white was not her favorite color.

"I suppose we could try to get in a little shopping so you can find something a little bit … nicer for dinner," Christina said to me in her rearview mirror.

"Don't worry, I brought a change of clothes," I said with a wink. I knew Christina well enough to know we wouldn't be eating dinner at a chain restaurant.

"What was that?" Aria asked, looking up from putting directions in the car's GPS.

"Nothing, let's roll," I said, kicking my feet up across the backseat. Christina scowled. I smiled in return.

The drive to Atlanta was long. Excruciatingly long, listening to Christina talk about her latest traveling adventures (You've never been to Switzerland?!) and the book she was writing as a result. "It's going to be a best seller, you just watch!" she exclaimed at one point. After she exhausted that topic, she moved on to discussing her latest investment opportunity. Christina had gotten into real estate, courtesy of Aria's uncle's financial backing, and you'd think she was the next Donald Trump the way she went on about her real estate holdings. I feigned sleep for most of it, so I didn't have to contribute much, but that didn't stop me from having to listen.

"I told them no. I wouldn't settle for less than five million. The name alone is worth at least that." Yada, yada, yada... She went on dropping this figure and that one. I had found that people who talked a lot about money didn't have as much as they wanted you to believe. It's the quiet ones driving the Lexuses who had it made, not the braggity-brag Christinas of the world.

We made it to the upscale bridal salon ten minutes before our appointment. Christina swung open the door and held it for Aria as if she were royalty. Me? I ran in front of them in search of a bathroom. I really had to pee and Christina had refused to stop saying, "I don't need to remind you that we're on a mission, ladies." Heaven forbid we were two minutes late. Christina even snapped at Aria when she agreed that stopping was a good idea. "If you didn't want to spend all day in the car, then we should've chartered a jet, or even Vince's helicopter would've worked." Aria reminded Christina that she was trying to not stress out Vince and that he might've needed the helicopter for business. "Then quit asking me when we're going to stop. We'll stop when we get there!" *Geez Louise.* Christina was ridiculous.

I joined them a few minutes later, sitting on the soft gray couch outside Aria's fitting room, while Christina bossed the consultant, Mallory, around.

"No, that's not one of the dresses I requested. The bodice

should be cut like this," she ordered, demonstrating by making a V on her neckline. "This one is all wrong."

"I'm sorry. This is the style number listed in your email," Mallory said.

"I don't care, it's not the right one." Christina brought up the dress she had wanted to see on her phone and showed it to the girl. "This one," she pointed to her screen, "not that one," and pointed to the dress on the rack. "See the difference?" Here we were, less than ten minutes into the appointment and the consultant was already being abused.

"I'm sure whatever you selected is great," I told Mallory while eying Christina as if to say, *"Knock it off, psycho."*

Christina rolled her eyes. "I can't handle this. I'll go find it." She walked away, dismissing both of us.

"Sorry about that. She's a bit of a perfectionist." Total control freak was more like it, but I was being polite. "Don't worry though, I've got your back. I'll keep her in check."

"Thanks, you have no idea how it can get," Mallory replied.

"Oh, I've watched enough reality TV to get the idea."

Aria came out in the first gown. Her scrunched-up face told it all. "Yeah, no," I said before she even got up on the pedestal.

Christina rushed right over. "But, look at the beading. The train. It's gorgeous," she insisted. The beading was ugly, the train way too long, and if by gorgeous she meant Aria looked like a marshmallow, then yeah, I could agree with her.

"Next!" I shouted. Aria smiled. I told myself that I would be as honest as possible while still being supportive. The goal was not to just get any dress, but one that Aria would love. I was there to make sure the second dress was even better than the first.

While Aria changed into another gown, I got up and peeked at the rest of the lineup Christina had personally selected. They all looked the same. All beaded, all fluffy, all white. All entirely wrong. This was going to be a disaster.

I walked over and knocked on Aria's door. "Hey girl, do you mind if I go pick out a few?"

Aria stuck her head out. She had on another ball gown, this one with so much tulle it was like a tutu on steroids. Aria blew her bangs out of her face. "Please do."

"Okay, give me a couple minutes. Be right back." My mission was clear. I pulled Mallory aside and asked her to show me something off the rack with color. That would be a start.

Mallory lead me to exactly what I was looking for. I found Aria's dress in a heartbeat. The form-fitting Marchesa mermaid gown was rose gold perfection with its gold embellishments laid over a blush dress and layer upon layer of soft, pleated tulle. Can you say dreamy? That dress was tulle done right. I had no doubt that Aria would look stunning in it. If I were getting married, that would be my dress. Aria would love it.

The moment she walked out of that fitting room wearing my pick, I knew I'd been right.

"I absolutely love it." Aria looked at herself in the mirror and was seriously glowing. Her frazzled nerves and blotchy complexion were totally calm. Aria was the happiest I had seen her in a long time. Looking at her made me happy. I thought for a second that she might even cry and, for once in my life, I was totally okay with it, if that tells you anything. The only person who wasn't feeling it was Christina.

"But it's pink!" she exclaimed as Aria said yes to the dress.

"Rose gold," I corrected her.

"I thought you wanted white?" she asked Aria, completely bewildered.

"Aria hates white." I said in a matter-of-fact voice. "Come on, let's go. Don't we have a manicure or shopping to do?"

Christina wasn't giving up that easily and begged Aria to try on a couple more dresses, "just to be sure," but Aria wasn't having it. She had found the one. "You should be happy," she was telling her, "I found my dress. Your plan worked, so thank you."

Christina perked up a bit at that and said in a smug voice, "Of course. After all, this whole day was my idea." I rolled my eyes hard at that one.

I treated Aria for her mani and pedi. I had been wanting to get her that gift certificate to the spa, which hadn't happened yet. This was the least I could do. The afternoon pampering session was heavenly, because I was in a separate room from Christina. Every now and then I could hear her say something along the lines of, "Well I know that when I was in Europe..." or "Real estate development is exhausting work. It's not easy counting millions!" I felt so sorry for her massage therapist. I'm not sure how much Christina tipped her, but it wasn't enough.

AFTER THE SPA, I had been right: dinner was at the Rolling Hills Country Club, which was part of Aria's uncle's plantation. Christina had spent summers there playing tennis and lounging by the pool while Aria worked as a life guard and beer girl. It was one of those rich brother, poor brother scenarios, with Aria's father being the poor one. No one could argue that Aria hadn't worked hard to elevate herself, regardless of how well she had married. She was already somebody before she and her first husband, Raja, said, "I do."

"Christopher, so good to see you," Christina said to the manager while we waited to be seated. Christopher was completely attentive to Christina, which she just ate up. Not saying he wasn't a nice guy, but I highly doubted he cared what Christina's summer travel plans were, especially to the extent Christina went on. Christopher's job looked exhausting.

The host came back and led us to our table.

The Club's dining room boasted dark woods, gold chandeliers, and burgundy carpeting. It was rich, and dark, and totally not my style. Give me natural light and bright whites any day.

A gold menu card had been placed at each place setting. I took a closer look and saw that Christina had arranged for a six-course meal to be served, highlights of which included gruyere and parmesan beignets, lobster bisque, arugula salad, prime rib, a cheese plate and chocolate mousse.

"My treat," Christina said, pleased as punch at my shocked expression, but she had read my expression all wrong. This dinner was just the sort of thing I expected from her. It was the chocolate mousse that had me wide-eyed. *Maybe we could skip to the dessert course first?*

It was close to nine PM by the time dinner was wrapping up. Once again, I was grateful to Inez for taking Captain Jack. No way my mom would've let him spend the night, well, not without giving me an earful first.

I was licking the back of my spoon, eyeing up Aria's mousse, wondering if she was going to eat it all, when a guy came over and tapped Aria on the shoulder.

"Oh, my goodness, Mike? How are you?"

Mike, who the heck is Mike? I thought to myself.

"I haven't seen you since what, college graduation?" Aria was saying.

Oh, my goodness, that Mike. As in the guy who broke my bestie's heart in college and who also stopped by my booth this past week at the farmers market. He had been the guy I hadn't been able to place. He looked so much more, I don't know, mature since the last time I saw him. Aria and Mike had been high school sweethearts turned college lovers, and it all went down in dramatic fashion when he called it quits. Aria and I had seen each other through a lot of different relationships and that breakup was brutal for her. I tried to help her find comfort in Ben & Jerry's but, even then, she turned to meditation and yoga.

"Ziva," Mike said.

"Long time no see." *Jerk.* I wasn't feeling as friendly now that I'd placed him.

"What are you up to?" Aria asked.

"Couple buddies are all in town. We just finished playing a round. Thought we'd grab a drink. Will you join us?"

I was thinking we should be getting back. I knew Christina would agree, but when I looked at Aria, I saw that she was seriously considering it. I wasn't sure what that was all about, but if she wanted a chance to catch up, then I was going to give it to her.

"Sure, why don't we," I said to Aria. Christina started to protest on cue, but we ignored her and followed Mike to the lounge.

Of course, I would have absolutely said no if I had known that one of his buddies was Whip McGovern.

"Ziva, did you follow me all the way here? I'm flattered."

"Whip, have you met Aria's cousin, Christina?" I shoved

Christina his way. She smiled, taking in his appearance. Whip was a handsome fella, and of course completely self-obsessed. Those two were made for one another.

We ordered a round of drinks and Aria and Mike got caught up, while Christina and I chatted up Whip. Wait, who am I kidding? I didn't chat with anyone. The conversation consisted of Whip talking about Whip while Christina talked about Christina. It was a case of anything you can do, I can do better. I could clearly see that I had been wrong. These two would never hit it off. The only difference was, where Whip claimed to have done something amazing like, "When I was in Nepal climbing Everest," to which Christina replied, "Everest? That's next on my list," I knew she was telling the truth. I'd bet the only mountain Whip had climbed was Space Mountain at Disney World.

I mentally checked out of their conversation and began to eavesdrop on Aria and Mike's behind me. Wow, now that conversation had me all sorts of flustered inside. I was sure Aria was a mess too.

"You know, I've been thinking about you a lot lately," Mike was saying.

"You have?" Aria seemed genuinely surprised. She hadn't said anything about Mike in a long time.

"I saw your engagement in the paper," Mike offered as way of explanation. Aria and Vince's engagement had been Page Six worthy, so I wasn't surprised it made the society pages in Atlanta.

"I even drove up to Port Haven last weekend hoping to run into you."

"You did?"

"I probably shouldn't have said anything, makes me look like an idiot, but I saw you tonight and I couldn't let it go. I think fate brought you here."

I thought it was a missing dress, but what did I know?

"It's just ... I'm such an idiot. I never told you I loved you. Very much. I realized it a bit too late. I'm sorry I didn't know it back then." I would've given anything to turn around and see the expression on his face. In fact, both of their faces.

"I loved you too. I told you that," Aria replied.

"I know, which is why I hate that I missed my chance. I'd do anything for another shot at us. Guess I shouldn't have waited so long."

Aria was speechless. I couldn't blame her.

"Any chance I'm not too late?"

I held my breath, honestly unsure what Aria would say. Yes, she loved Vince now, but it had to be hard to think straight when your ex-boyfriend, the one you had thought was "the one," was standing in front of you spilling his heart out.

I couldn't resist and I had to turn around. I pretended to look at the television playing over their heads. Truthfully, I was staring at Mike's puppy-dog eyes.

Aria finally spoke, "That's really sweet, Mike, but I'm really happy right now and can't wait to marry my fiancé." Aria shrugged her shoulders. "Sorry."

Mike looked defeated. "That's okay. I knew it was a long shot, but I had to ask."

"It was nice seeing you though. Glad we got to catch up," Aria said, trying to make light of the situation.

"Yeah, me too. Congrats, then, I guess."

"Thanks."

A couple beats of awkward silence hung in the air.

"Will you excuse me?" Aria said. Mike nodded of course and Aria walked away from him. I did the same, leaving my conversation and chasing after her.

We met up in the ladies room.

"You okay, girl? I was totally eavesdropping."

"Yeah, wow. I wasn't expecting all that. Joining them hadn't been a good idea."

"Sorry about that. I thought you wanted to."

"I had, but it wasn't smart."

"He doesn't have you second guessing Vince, does he?"

"Maybe a little. I guess not so much second guessing, but more like playing the "what ifs.""

I could see that.

"But then honestly, I just think that if Mike and I hadn't broken up, then I would've never met Raja and had Arjun. Thinking about my little boy makes Mike just a guy from my past."

"Girl, your head is in a better place than mine would be."

"I've had a long time to think about Mike and, since him, I've been shown what love truly is. I'm not sure Mike knows what that's like."

"True. So, what now? You ready to bounce?" I asked.

"Definitely. Let's nab Christina and get the heck out of here."

hursday morning meant business. Since I lost yesterday, I'd have to work my tail off all day to get caught up. The security system I had ordered a couple of days ago was delivered first thing, and I planned to install it immediately. The system came with a camera, a couple window sensors, and a motion detector. It also synched with my phone, so I could keep an eye on my place when I wasn't there and receive notifications if anything was triggered. My apartment wasn't Fort Knox, but it would do. I was driving over to Inez's to pick up Captain Jack and then headed home to install it when a county line rang.

"Honey girl, what's taking you so long?" Mrs. J. asked when I answered. You'd think I was late picking her up for church. I shouldn't have been surprised; Mrs. J. was annoyed when her beauty products weren't delivered on time. Sitting in a jail cell must have been driving her nuts.

"Sorry, Mrs. J., I'm working on it."

"Well, work faster. If I don't get out of here soon, I'm going to organize one of them hunger strikes on account of the food being horrendous. Don't even get me started on their pecan pie. Now that should be a crime."

Glad to hear she's staying out of trouble. "Hey, what do you know about Bob McGovern or his son Whip?"

"Bob was a fool. Talked a lot, but never got much done. Of course, he didn't have to being he was a McGovern."

"Come again?"

"Old money and plenty of it, or there used to be. Heard funds are low. What's this got to do with getting me out of here?"

"Just another angle I'm working. You know Whip's running for mayor."

"And Bob hated Humphrey. That's good 'sug, real good."

"Thanks. I just don't have any evidence yet, only motive." Evidence seemed to be in short supply around here. I added "collect evidence" on my growing list of items to-do.

Someone knocked at my front door and I told Mrs. J. that I'd check in with her later. I really should've tried out my new security camera before answering the door because when I did, I opened it to none other than Whip McGovern himself. He stood on my doorstep with a bouquet of white roses in one hand and an invitation in the other.

"Oh, hi, I wasn't expecting anyone." I looked past him, expecting to see someone else with him, but he was alone. That surprised me. Knowing Whip and his ego, I wouldn't put it past him to hire his own paparazzi. "What can I do for you?" I really didn't want to invite him in.

"You took off yesterday without saying goodbye. I figured that had to be a mistake," he said, laughing at his own words as if they were a pun of a joke. We had taken off rather quickly last night. Christina had had no problem leaving once she mentally declared herself the winner. "He's never even been to Spain!" She told us on the way home. That was all I had heard because, thankfully, I fell asleep shortly after that comment and slept the rest of the way home.

"Not a mistake. So again, what can I do for you?"

"Well, I was just thinking to myself, "Whip, you should have a date to Saturday's Governor's Ball and then I thought, who would love to join me? And your name came right to mind. I'm sure you'd be honored."

No, no I would not. Good thing it was also Aria's wedding day. I doubted he would've accepted that I was washing my hair, or more like, I'd rather eat dirt. "Aria's wedding is on Saturday."

"You can't skip it?" His face was totally serious.

I looked at Whip like he had two heads. "She's my best friend. Plus, I don't think my boyfriend would appreciate it."

Whip waved that away. "He wouldn't care. It's not every night you get to have dinner with the governor."

"I wasn't talking about the governor part." Whip ignored me and proceeded to hand me both the flowers and envelope. "Here, why don't you keep those, or better yet, give them to someone else who wants them," I said.

"I bought them for you. I insist." He tried to hand the flowers to me once more.

I grabbed my car keys off the hook by the front door and stepped out of my apartment, shutting the door behind me and forcing Whip to backup.

"Sorry, but I really have to run." I had promised Aria that I'd help her with wedding stuff today as well. The plan was that I'd meet her at Park Place Hotel this afternoon to survey the damage of her reception venue and go from there. Truth be told, I still had forty minutes until I was supposed to meet her, but that was irrelevant. Whip didn't budge, but I didn't care. I scooted past him and bounded down the stairs to my truck. I didn't really care if he stood

there all day. I had a security camera now. I'd know if he
tried something fishy.

I DUG through my purse and called Detective Roxy from my
truck. I wanted to tell her about the McGoverns and see if
she could piece things together from her end. Wouldn't that
have just made life easier? Of course, she didn't answer, so I
left her a message.

Since I had a few minutes to spare, I drove to the post
office and decided to rent a PO box instead of having all my
deliveries sent downstairs to the antiques shop. It might be
totally inconvenient popping into the post office all the time,
but at least I could be sure my mail would be safe until I
figured out what the heck was going on, and I wouldn't have
to bother Kathleen every day. My wallet would thank
me too.

With that task completed, I headed to Park Place. I was
majorly hoping the venue wouldn't be all that bad and we
could check one thing off Aria's ever-growing list of
disasters.

It turned out to be worse than I imagined.

I should've known it was going to be a mess when the
wedding planner insisted we have tea first. Park Place was
known for hosting a formal afternoon tea. The tea room was
a sight, with its Waterford chandeliers, delicate floral china
and crisp white lines. The only thing we were missing were
the fancy-shmancy hats. At least my shorts were designer. I
could've totally dug the European vibe if I wasn't getting
more suspicious by the minute. Don't get me wrong, I loved
a good tea party, especially those lemon scones and miniature cucumber and dill sandwiches, but the extra VIP treat-

ment was making me wary. I tried to brush it off. Aria was, after all, marrying Vincent Delgado, Savannah's most eligible and wealthiest bachelor; not to mention, most people thought he was corrupt as could be, a reputation that he helped facilitate. I tried to keep that in mind, which is why for over an hour, I let the staff of Park Place fuss over my bestie and bring out scones and sandwiches, this special tea and that one for her to sample. They even capped off the service with a little Earl Grey-infused truffle. Personally, I thought tea belonged in the pot, but I never turned down a truffle.

Finally, we were invited to follow the wedding coordinator to the Grande Ballroom. As soon as I saw the giant floor fans, I knew we were in trouble. We walked through the double doors and directly into chaos. Workers were everywhere—replacing the dance floor, steaming carpets, and pulling wallpaper down. A woman, who I assumed to be a designer, was holding paint swatches next to folds of material, apparently trying to decide which paint color matched the new curtains.

"All this for a little water damage, huh?" I said to the wedding coordinator. I would've said it to Aria, but she looked a bit catatonic, standing in the middle of the room, eyes wide, mouth open.

"It was more than just a little water. More than one alarm was pulled. The entire system was activated," the coordinator said to me, and then turned to Aria and added, "I know this looks bad, but I promise everything will be perfect on Saturday." I wondered if she felt bad lying like that because I was fairly optimistic, and even I couldn't see how this was going to be perfect.

Aria shared my skepticism and told the coordinator so.

"I completely understand. If you want to cancel, your

deposit will be fully refunded and there won't be any penalties for breaking contract." *I should hope not.*

Aria told the coordinator that she'd get back to her later that day. We took one last look at the disaster and walked out. We started winding our way down the halls back toward the front of the hotel when that goofy guy with the fedora ran right into me. I think he was trying to split Aria and me, but it didn't work. I didn't fall, but I did stumble backwards a few steps.

"My apologies. I'm so sorry. Can't stay. Gotta go. Gotta catch 'em." The man never stopped moving.

"That guy is seriously nuts. Are you okay?" Aria asked.

"Yeah, I'm fine." I rubbed my shoulder where he had bumped me. "Anyway, where were we?"

"About to discuss my reception."

Now, most girls probably would've tried to reassure her friend that everything was going to be okay and that the ballroom would be awesome, but I'm a realist. "Girl, that place is a mess. What's Plan B?"

"I know. I don't need this," Aria shook her head.

"I hate to ask, but do you want me to call Christina?" She probably had alternatives all laid out in a spread sheet. I could picture the little neat rows and tabs now.

"No, I know she's trying to help, but man, she's just one more stressor. I don't think I can handle another one of her great ideas."

"I feel you, but it could be worse."

"How so? Because this seems about as bad as it can get."

"Well, you could be having second thoughts about Vince." I thought about her seeing Mike again. "Let me tell you, the where and when can be easily changed. The who, not so much."

"That's supposed to make me feel better?"

"What I'm trying to say is, as long as you're sure about Vince, then the rest of the details shouldn't matter."

"Okay, that's true, but we still need to find some place to have the reception."

"True, which is why you need to call Vince. He's a genius businessman. I'm sure he can sort this out."

"Speaking of feeling better...," Aria motioned down the hall. Walking in front of us was Mayor Potts. He had a little extra spring in his step and did, in fact, look like he felt better. He stopped to knock on a door, and I was going to call to get his attention when Suzanne opened the door, wearing an ivory silk robe with a glass of champagne in each hand. I pulled Aria into an entryway just down the hall and across from them. Mayor Potts took the glass and gave Suzanne a kiss to end all kisses and closed the door behind them.

"What was that?" Aria said.

Well, well. "That explains the pep in his step," I replied, still shocked. I never would've guessed the mayor was cheating on Paulette with her best friend. In terms of the case, I wasn't about to jump to any conclusions. The last murder I solved taught me that perceptions were rarely what they seemed.

18

On the way home, Aria and I couldn't stop talking about what we had witnessed.

"I wonder if he was cheating on Paulette the whole time?" I asked.

"Is Suzanne married?"

"No, I thought she was, but it turns out the guy, who I thought was her husband, is actually her stepson."

"Her husband..."

"Passed away, but hopefully she was nicer to him than she is to his son."

"Really? She sounds lovely."

"I know, right? Jeffery's tall, thin, geeky sort of guy, but really nice. Of course, Suzanne thinks he's a hapless fool. I don't see it at all."

"Maybe she just hates men," Arai offered.

"Well, we know she doesn't hate the mayor."

"He went right for it."

"Yeah he did." I shook my head.

"So, what are you thinking? Suzanne killed Paulette?"

"I don't know. Don't forget, Humphrey was poisoned too.

That part doesn't make sense. She's obviously quite fond of him, or at least part of him." We both chuckled. "And then you have the McGoverns."

"Yeah, Whip's a narcissist if I ever met one."

"You can say that again. I didn't even tell you that he stopped by my place this afternoon."

"What?!" I filled Aria in on our little conversation.

"So yeah, do narcissists have homicidal tendencies? Because if so, I could see him being the killer all day long, especially if it meant him getting what he wanted. Plus, he has a pretty strong motive for wanting the mayor dead."

"But not for Paulette."

"True. I already thought about that. I still don't have an answer."

"And you don't think Mrs. J. is somehow responsible for all this?"

"I seriously don't. She didn't like Paulette, but there are a lot of people she doesn't like and they're still alive and kicking. But I have a feeling a lot of people would like to see Mrs. J. locked up for good, the way she's always sticking her nose in everyone's business."

"Very true. She's got the dirt on everyone."

"Exactly. She seems like an easy person to frame. It was no secret that she and Paulette hated one another. The other person I keep coming back to is Vicki Kline. She's Paulette and Suzanne's childhood friend, or rather wanna-be friend. She's also an expert botanist. I took her poisonous-plants class Monday, and let me just say, wow."

"That good, huh?"

"She could definitely kill you with a plant or two."

"What's your gut say?"

"My gut says there's more to Vicki's story. I can't figure out why, especially now that she's a grown woman, she's still hanging around Suzanne and Paulette. Like, what's the draw?"

"You want to take a closer look?"

"I think we should."

"Okay, I'll give you an hour, but then we have to get back to fixing my wedding. Deal?"

"Deal."

Aria did a white-pages search on Vicki and easily found where she lived. The internet can be freaky like that. I was certain that's how Whip found me this afternoon. Vicki's house was located across the street from the elementary school. She lived in a pretty yellow bungalow with little picket-fence accents and an impressive front garden. I might be flower illiterate, but I knew a nice rose garden when I saw one.

I wasn't quite sure how this was going to go down, seeing it was the middle of the afternoon. We swung by my apartment on the way to pick up Captain Jack and for me to put together a little summer Beauty Secrets gift bag as a cover. I included a bottle of coconut sunscreen, cooling lip balm, and a pair of flip flops in my employer's signature violet hue.

The plan was for me to drop Aria off further down the street and have her walk Captain Jack to the school playground. From there, she could keep an eye out while I looked around, and she'd text me if needed. Meanwhile, I parked in front of Vicki's house and crossed my fingers that she wasn't home.

Luck appeared to be on my side. After ringing the bell and waiting the socially appropriate thirty seconds, I peered inside Vicki's foyer window. Her front sitting room and entry way looked as tidy as could be. A couple of books were stacked on her front entry table, a lacy doily underneath them with a single rose in a vase beside them. I couldn't make out all the details, but the top one had a leaf on it and the word "Medicinal" in the title. A bit strange, but not all that surprising, knowing Vicki's passion for plants.

I left the beauty gift bag on the front porch with my card inside, and looked over my shoulder. Aria was having a seat on a playground swing, Captain Jack sat in her lap. From across the street, I could hardly see any pink left in his coat. I stepped off the porch and walked further up the driveway toward the detached, single-car garage. Again, the garage didn't house anything all that exciting. Several bags of potting soil, a work bench, stacks of planters, and a vintage Coca Cola machine took up most of the space. Of course, the sight of the soda machine had me crushing on Finn. My guy loved his cola. And I liked that he had a tendency to drink it with his shirt off.

A decorative waist-high white fence surrounded the yard. The gate wasn't locked, so I pushed open the metal latch and followed the stone path around to the back of the house. If I had thought the front gardens were beautiful, the back gardens were spectacular. So many colors and textures blended together, it reminded me of a painting. Her landscape even featured a bubbling fountain with a koi pond smack dab in the middle of her yard. It was very Zen like and I would've loved to stay for a while had I not been on a recon mission.

Tucked in the corner of the yard, I spotted a tool shed. My mouth got all tingly like it does when I eat too much sugar, and I thought I was finally on to something. I quickly crossed the yard and peeked inside the side window of the shed and did a double take. *Holy guacamole, Vicki grows a lot of wacky tobacky!* Marijuana wasn't the only surprising find. Vicki also had beakers filled with various powders and liquids lined up on her workbench, dozens of dried flowers and herbs bundled together and hanging from the ceiling, and notebook after notebook stacked on a bookshelf titled "research." Off to the side, sitting on a shelf was a microscope, rubber gloves, and brown glass bottles with cork stoppers. A white lab coat hung on a hook next to it. I may have just found my evidence. I took out my phone and was going to snap some pics when Aria texted me two words: Vicki's home.

Sweet sugar, now is not the time.

I quickly looked left and right for a place to hide. Vicki's car pulled up the driveway and I threw myself flat on the ground with an oomph. My shorts would be sporting some major grass stains later, but I didn't care. I scurried as fast as I could, keeping my head down, to the other side of the shed and ran behind it, squishing myself between the shed and the small fence.

I should've been looking in front of me and not over my shoulder. That was a major mistake. I ran right into a skunk. As in, I almost stepped on the little guy. I'm not sure which of us was more freaked out. I gave a shriek and leapt over him, jumping the fence like it was a hurdle, while he sprayed. I landed in a summersault-like fashion in the neighbor's yard and stood up to run from the little bugger, unsure if I had been hit or not. The neighbor's dog barked and I looked up to see a ginormous mastiff charging toward me. I kicked up my speed, jumped over a kiddie pool, around a trampoline and was about to run through a hedge when I totally slipped in a ginormous pile of dog poo. I swear I went airborne for a second, flying high in the sky along with chunks of dog poo, before landing flat on my back, the air completely pushed out of my lungs.

OOOOF! I lay there gasping for air, unable to suck any in, my diaphragm completely forgetting how to work. I rolled onto my side in the fetal position and felt a big, slobbery wet dog kiss across my face and into my hair. *Oh gross.* The mastiff continued to lick me, I think to make sure that I was okay. Either that, or to slobber me to death. Drool stuck in my hair and ran down my neck. It was disgusting.

After a minute, when I could finally breathe, I rolled over onto all fours and looked up at the furry beast. I swear he smiled.

ARIA LOOKED HORRIFIED when she spotted me. I had walked over and met her on the playground. My shorts were grass-stained, shoes and backside were smeared with dog poop, my hair was styled with essence of dog, and the overall aroma of skunk clung to my body. I would've smelled better after an afternoon of dumpster diving.

Captain Jack, excitedly ran toward me on his leash; but once he reached me and took in a whiff, he sneezed and pawed at his nose.

Aria shook her head and backed away. "No way, girl. I am not riding with you."

"It's not that bad." I looked down at my disheveled, stinky self. "Okay, it is that bad. Just do me a favor. Run over to Vicki's and get my truck. I'll stay here and hop in the back." I figured if I lay down in the bed of my truck, no one would see me and maybe I'd air out a bit. "Please? Pretty please with sugar on top?"

Aria looked like she was ready to bolt.

"Who found the perfect wedding dress for you?" I reminder her in a sugary voice.

I had Aria and she knew it. "You so owe me, girl."

"Would you like a hug?" I outstretched my arms.

"Don't you dare!" Aria backed up while saying the words, and then turned and jogged across the playground to fetch my truck.

I WENT home and took the longest shower of my life, complete with a baking soda and peroxide scrub to help get the stench off. I had peeled off my clothes the second I got home and chucked them in the trash, throwing the bag on my front porch. I wasn't ready to part with my Converses yet, even if they did take a direct hit from the skunk. I put those in a separate grocery bag on my porch next to the trash while I debated what to do with them. *Let's see someone steal that*, I thought. It would serve them right.

This evening was the dinner party at Mrs. DeVine's. If I hadn't already told her I'd be there, and if she wasn't my financial backer, I would've backed out. As it was, I could only hope I didn't smell too awful.

Once I was cleaned up, I switched over to wedding planning and googled "online flower packages" to see what we could get shipped in by Friday. From the looks of it, you could buy anything online for a price. Good thing Vince was paying. I text a couple links and images to Aria to see what she thought. Neither one of us had much experience in floral design, but I was thinking that if we got the blooms in, we could pay a florist to arrange them. Although, maybe not Claire or Betsy.

Then I looked up "how to make a wedding cake," you know, incase Mrs. J. was still in jail come Friday. Just looking at the pictures, I decided that wasn't happening. I was more of an eater than a baker. I sighed and tried to think about what Aria really wanted in a cake. *Maybe Sweet Thangs could make some carrot cupcakes with organic cream cheese frosting or something along those lines.* The healthier they could make it, the more Aria would love it.

I sat and debated if I should just call Sweet Thangs or run over. It didn't take much to get me to stop in to my favorite sweets shop. I stared at my phone, thinking about it, and on cue, it rang. I had an incoming FaceTime call from a number I didn't recognize. Normally, I wouldn't answer such calls, but with Finn out to sea ... I never knew what number he'd call me on. I pulled my hair over my shoulder, smoothed out my shirt, and answered. Whip McGovern's face filled the screen. Yikes. I pulled the phone away. He was a little too close. He hadn't realized that I had answered. He was still checking himself out in the camera, running his fingers through his hair and making sure nothing was stuck in his teeth.

I went to hit *end* when he saw we were connected. "Just wanted to check in and see if you'd changed you mind. I know it's a tempting offer." Whip just couldn't drop it. I had a feeling women didn't tell him no all that often.

"Yeah, no, definitely didn't change my mind."

"I heard the pastry chef is amazing," Whip countered.

What the heck, is this guy spying on me? I'm ashamed to say that I did think about it, for like a millisecond before, once again, telling him that I wasn't interested and he'd be better off ringing someone else up. I hung up before he could say another word. I had to get ready for tonight.

19

J arrived at Mrs. DeVine's just after six PM. I hadn't felt like dressing up, but I couldn't show up looking like a bum either. I decided to wear a red-patterned cotton romper with leather, heeled sandals and gold hooped earrings. Tonight's party was a garden-themed event and my wardrobe choice was perfect. The air was warm, the humidity had lifted, and I found myself wondering what Mrs. DeVine treated her yard with to keep the mosquitoes away. For whatever reason, the suckers usually ate me alive if I didn't plan ahead, and tonight was one such occasion.

Mrs. DeVine greeted me with a hug and kiss on each cheek. "Wonderful to see you, darling," she said.

It could've just been my imagination, but I swear she sniffed my hair. I hoped she picked up the subtle grapefruit notes in my shampoo and not the lasting scent of *eau de dog*.

"You too." I swept my hair over one shoulder.

"I can't wait to stop by and see our new retail space." Mrs. DeVine announced the last part over her shoulder so a handful of guests heard her.

I gave a non-committal, "Uh-huh." I couldn't wait to see it either, wherever "it" ended up being. Cassandra still hadn't called back. I was going to have to quickly locate a new space if that one fell through. Mrs. DeVine eyed me expectantly, and I was about to spill the beans when none other than Whip McGovern interrupted us.

"You didn't tell me you'd be here tonight." He had come up from behind and I almost didn't move fast enough to avoid his kiss on the cheek. Whip laughed it off and whispered into my neck, "Playing hard to get, are we? I like it," before greeting Mrs. DeVine. "It was nice of you to throw this party for me tonight. I'm honored. I see you even made my favorite—crab cakes." It was hard to tell if he was joking. Mrs. DeVine's expression faltered for just a second, but it was enough for me to see that she shared my impression of the guy. Unfortunately, she didn't know that and excused herself so Whip and I could, "enjoy ourselves."

"Now, where were we?" Whip said when she left.

"Listen, I'm flattered and all, but this," I motioned between us, "it's not happening."

"Not yet."

"Not ever."

"You say that now."

For the love of all things chocolate, this man is hopeless. I thought about smacking him across the face, or spilling my drink on him, but I knew that would only encourage him. Instead, I played to his ego. "You know, I might change my mind, but the truth of the matter is, you deserve someone better than me." That caught his attention. "I'm just a small business owner with not much to call my own. You need someone with a much more impressive résumé. Someone who deserves to be the mayor's wife ... No, make that, the *governor's* wife, or maybe even the First Lady." I thought I might have gone a little too far with that last part, but Whip had stars in his eyes. Man, he was totally delusional. I knew he was picturing it now.

Whip turned serious and coughed to clear his throat. "That must have been painful for you to admit, but I see now that you're right. I do deserve someone with an equal pedigree to my own."

"And aspirations," I added.

"No, no, we don't need her to try and outdo me now," Whip said, and chuckled as if he found himself hilarious again.

Oh brother.

I watched him survey the gardens to see if such a woman would appear.

"Well, good luck with that." I said, with a fake smile. Whip paid no attention to me. I walked away from him as quickly as I could and ended up walking right into Suzanne Butterfield.

"Oh sorry, I was just—"

"Running away?"

"Exactly."

"I can't stand that man." *Well, there's a shocker.* Another man who Suzanne hated. I looked behind her, half expecting to see Mayor Potts. I wondered how much longer their relationship was going to stay secret. I spotted Jeffery instead. He came up and stood next to Suzanne. She completely ignored him. I greeted him with a smile and a friendly "hello". Only then did Suzanne look over her shoulder to see who I could possibly be talking to.

She changed the subject. "So, did you get a chance to try my honey? It's the best," she said the last word all sing-songy.

"Not yet, but it's on my must-do list, and soon." *Could*

whoever killed Paulette turn themselves in? It would really save me some time and let me focus on my own life again.

"Well, have you at least tried the baklava? It was made with my honey. I was just telling Mrs. DeVine how much I love helping area business out."

Does baklava have chocolate in it? I didn't think so, which is why I had no intention of trying it. I did however plan on having another drink. I paid homage to my heritage and nabbed a piña colada from the waiter when he stopped by. I took a sip of the sweet rum cocktail and, for just a moment, I was transported to Flamenco Beach, with its soft, white sand and calm, crystal waters. I closed my eyes and could almost hear the waves rushing in. I needed a vacation in the worst way. Sun, sand, Finn by my side. I was ready to book it today. *I wonder what Finn would say?* If I was feeling brave, I'd mention it to him when he got back. I swear, I was a total badass until it came to relationships.

Since I wasn't on vacation now, I did the mingling thing, chatting with this person and that, skirting around Mrs. Devine's inquiry on how business was going. "It's been very busy!" I replied, a little too enthusiastically. Once again, I didn't offer any details, and thankfully another guest joined the conversation, sparing me from having to elaborate. I *had* been very busy, just not in the way she might have thought. I could've continued to work the garden and make some new contacts, but my heart just wasn't in it.

I was thinking about my next move when I spotted Vicki walking toward me. If I could've disappeared right then and there, I would've. I prayed she hadn't seen me fleeing her backyard. I tried to think up a story quick, like maybe Captain Jack got loose and I chased him through her backyard?

"Hey, I wasn't expecting to see you here," I said when she reached me.

"Oh yeah, Cynthia and I go way back. She's a flower lover like me."

"That's nice."

"It is. Sorry I missed you earlier today."

"Er... my dog... um, I..." My face must've looked panicked.

"The beauty bag, on my doorstep."

"Oh, yes, yes, yes, that's right. Sorry, it's been a long day." *Major understatement.* "I just wanted to drop that off and let you try out a couple products." *And see what secrets you had hidden.* "You'll have to let me know what you think."

Vicki assured me she would and then I excused myself from the conversation. Last thing I needed was to slip up and let her know that I had been snooping.

I looked toward the dessert table and saw a woman about my age busting her butt, trying to keep everything stocked and looking *just so*. I knew a girl boss when I saw one. *Now, she is someone I should network with.* My bet was she was a new caterer on the scene, and tonight was Mrs. DeVine's way of introducing her. That was just the type of thing she did. If that was the case, tonight would be huge for her. Mrs. DeVine had that type of star power. Most caterers would kill for an opportunity to host one of her parties.

"Hey there, need a hand?" I asked. The caterer was holding a baking sheet in one hand and arranging appetizers on a plate with the other.

"No, thanks though, I've got it," she said with a smile.

"I'm Ziva, by the way. I saw you over here working your tail off and thought I'd come over and say hi."

"Megan Kennedy, and thanks. I think everything's going okay, right?"

I looked around and surveyed the crowd. Everyone seemed to be eating and enjoying themselves, maybe a bit too much. *Are those two making out over there?* Someone else appeared to be hunting for coins in Mrs. Devine's fountain. *Maybe it's time to cut off the alcohol, buddy.* I tried to refocus and assure Megan that everything was fabulous.

"Good to know. After my last gig, I need everything to be perfect." I looked at Megan and waited for her to elaborate.

"I had my first wedding at Park Place and, let's just say, it didn't go as planned. I'm not sure I'll get booked there again anytime soon."

"Oh, the fire alarm..." *How could I forget?* "My girlfriend's supposed to have her reception there Friday, and we're not sure if the ballroom's going to be repaired in time. She's super stressed out."

"Yeah, here's the thing, they tried blaming me for it at first. I mean, I get it, a fire alarm goes off and you blame the cook, but that's not even remotely possible. The only open flame I had were those little heaters that keep food warm. There's no way the chaffing fuel would cause the fire sensors to go off."

"They blamed you? That's crazy."

"They tried to, until I realized that I caught the real culprit on camera."

"You did not? That's awesome. How'd you manage that?"

"I was taking a quick promo video, and you can clearly see someone pulling the alarm in the background. I turned the video over to the hotel the next day. The only problem is, no one knows who she is."

"Can I see it?"

"Yeah, of course. I wanted to ask around and see if anyone recognized her. Only problem with being new is that's kind of hard to do."

Megan flipped through her phone, and then handed it over to me. I watch as a video played across the screen. Up-close shots of the wedding cake, panning over to the bacon-wrapped asparagus and crostini's topped with goat-cheese hors d'oeuvres. The food did look delicious, which reminded me that I should ask Megan what her plans were for Friday night. As far as I knew, Aria still needed a caterer.

"There, right there." Megan pointed to a figure moving along the back wall. I peered a little closer and gasped. *I'd recognize those stupid little braids anywhere.* I watched in a mixture of amusement and horror as Christina reached over and nonchalantly pulled the fire alarm. Megan then must've dropped the phone. I could hear the siren going off in the back ground before the video cut off.

"Then, less than a minute later, another alarm goes off and then another. The girl must've pulled a couple more on her way out," Megan said. I remembered the wedding coordinator saying that the entire system wouldn't have been activated, unless it was a multi-sensor trigger.

"I know her."

"You do?" Megan's face lite up.

"Yep, and I'll make sure she pays. Here, do me a favor, text me that video and I'm going to go hunt her down." I had a feeling Christina was behind all of Aria's wedding disasters.

I turned around just in time to see Whip running buck naked around Mrs. DeVine's back yard. I slapped my hand over my mouth. Whip was shouting something about being king of the world, but from where I stood, it looked more like the prince of the pea pod, if you know what I'm saying. If I were his campaign advisor, I'd be telling him to keep his pants on at all further public appearances. Out of nowhere, that goofy guy with the trench coat and fedora jumped down from a tree, took photos of Whip, and ran across the backyard, through the hedge.

I looked around, expecting everyone to be shocked, but truth be told, they were acting kooky too. Even Mrs. DeVine seemed goofy. "My arms, they're all tingly!" she happily explained. Suzanne might have supplied the honey for the baklava, but I had a feeling Vicki supplied the bud for the brownies. Seriously, they were all tripping out.

Megan was the only other person who seemed horrified. "I'm out of here," I told her. I had no idea what was going on, but I did not want to be a part of it.

"I'm right behind you," Megan said as she started packing up.

Before leaving, I promised her I'd pass on the video and the girl's name directly to the police, and then call her tomorrow and let her know how it all went.

"Excellent. Thank you so much," she said.

"No, trust me, thank *you*."

20

I called Aria the minute I reached my truck. She answered right away.

"Hey, girlie, got a minute?" I asked.

"I'm about to walk into Nine's and hand my wedding over to Christina. I'm done. She can just take over and do her thing."

"Don't!"

"What? Why?"

"I'll explain when I get there. Just order yourself a drink," *maybe two*, "and I'll be there in a jiffy."

I drove fast on most occasions, and tonight was no exception. I thought about all the drama Aria had put up with this last week and all the stress Christina had caused— the missing dress, the cancelled flowers, the ruined reception venue... I was willing to bet there hadn't even been a catering issue, Christina just made that last part up. I was steaming by the time I pulled in front of Nine's. Part of me wanted to ask Christina to step outside, but I thought of my mother again. Bar fighting always got her so worked up.

I walked into the lounge and spotted Aria and Christina,

sitting at the long booth that ran the length of the side wall. Well, Christina was sitting in the booth. Aria sat on a chair across from her. I pulled a chair over from the next table and joined their two-top, effectively blocking Christina from being able to make a run for it, and cementing my position next to my bestie. Christina had her notes neatly placed in front of them along with color swatches, seating charts, and pictures of flower arrangements.

"Hey, girls," I said with a little wave. Christina looked surprised to see me. *Perfect.* Aria hadn't tipped her off. Christina recovered quickly though and replied with the fakest smile ever. *Keep smiling,* I thought. I noticed that one of the tiny braids that zig zagged up her head had come loose and fallen across her face. For once, her hair didn't look perfect. If she was frazzled now, I was excited to see how she would be feeling in a few moments. *This is going to be fun.*

"Sorry to crash your little shindig here, but I need to show Aria something. It'll just take a minute." I handed my phone over to Aria and smiled. "It gets really good at about a minute fifteen." I turned my attention to Christina. "So, you're taking over the wedding plans now?"

"Well, somebody has too." Christina's expression turned smug.

"I don't know; it looks like you had plenty of time to think all this through." I motioned to the wedding plans spread out on the table.

"I work fast."

"Uh-huh." *Yes, you do.*

"Right there." I pointed to the figure on camera. Aria gave a little gasp and I knew she recognized Christina.

"And bingo," I said to Aria as we watched Christina pull the alarm.

Christina tried to look over at what we were watching. "What's that?"

I folded my hands and placed my elbows on the table, leaning forward and batting my eyes. "Just a little video I found from last week's disaster at Park Place."

The color drained from Christina's face.

"You're busted."

"I didn't. It was an accident. I just—" Christina looked side to side. On one side of her was a wall, on the other side was me.

"Christina! What's wrong with you? Seriously!" Aria shouted.

Christina stammered some more, threw in a swear word or two, and then crawled under the table and tried to make a break for it. I meant to grab her shoulder, but grabbed one of her braids instead. Christina screamed and pivoted around. She lunged for me, arms outstretched as if she were going to choke me. I flipped my hand upside down and grabbed her by the wrist, twisting it over. Her purse had been on her arm and the contents of it spilled out onto the floor. I wasn't paying any attention, but Aria was. She picked up a little green bottle and handed it to me. I dropped Christina's wrist. The bottle had a picture of a poison ivy plant on it, which I could now identify, thanks to Vicki's class. Above the image was a giant warning label. *Sweet sugar! Christina was the one tampering with my products.* Christina turned and snatched the bottle out of my hands. I readily let her have it. She wasn't expecting that and, in her aggression, she slipped and hit the ground. Glass crunched underneath her and I took a giant step back. Christina rolled over and her entire shirt was soaked in poison ivy oil.

"No one touch her!" I shouted to all the lookie-loos standing around. Aria grabbed a pitcher of ice water from a nearby table and doused her in it. Christina shrieked. Aria looked up at me as if to say, *"What? Bad idea?"* I shrugged my shoulders. Worked for me.

I wasn't quite sure how it all was going to go down, but I didn't expect cops! A couple of the boys in blue walked in a minute later and tried to figure out what had happened. Apparently, a few fingers were pointed at me and, before I could talk my way out of it, my butt was sitting in the back of a cop car. This wasn't a first. Hopefully, my mother wouldn't find out. Finn would probably find it hilarious. Before the door was shut, I did manage to say, "Call Detective Roxy and tell her I solved the poison-ivy case."

Thankfully, the cops listened to me, or maybe it was Aria. I could see her flapping her arms and pointing at me in the police car, trying to get them to let me go. Detective Roxy showed up not too long after and opened the squad-car door. I stepped out as I saw Christina ducking into the back of another.

Detective Roxy was in biker-chick apparel, black leather pants with a matching vest. She was a bigger badass than I was. I just had to do something about that lavender lipstick she was sporting. *Blech.*

We stood on the sidewalk for a few minutes while I filled her in and showed her the video.

"Mind texting that to me?" the detective asked.

"No problem. Like I said, I got it from the caterer, Megan Kennedy. You're going to want to chat with her, too. I'll text you her info." I took a mental note to give Megan a heads up that Detective Roxy would be getting in touch with her.

"Hey, not sure what's going on with the whole Paulette case, but I've been doing some digging." Detective Roxy did the eyeing-me-up thing again. "Anyway, you might want to look into Vicki Kline ... well, her gardening shed, anyway." I left it at that, not wanting to incriminate myself.

"Oh! And Whip McGovern? Yeah, his family has a beef with the mayor. Not sure if you'd heard."

"Anything else?" Detective Roxy seemed amused.

"Nope. Am I good to go?"

"As long as you're not planning on doing anymore investigating."

"Not tonight." I winked and ran over to meet Aria. She had been chatting away on her cell phone while I was, let's say, detained. Christina had since been taken away.

"What's the game plan, yo?" I was willing to pull an all-nighter and help Aria re-plan her wedding. We had less than forty-eight hours until the scheduled *I do's* and I was fully up to the challenge.

"Vince is on it," Aria said, putting her phone back in her purse.

"You told him?" Aria nodded her head. "About time."

"Oh, shut up."

"No, seriously, I'm glad you filled him in."

"Me too. I guess these things don't stress him out like they do me. I'm actually going to go meet up with him now. Is that cool?"

"Yeah of course. Absolutely." I gave my bestie a hug and told her to call me soon and let me know if I could help with anything.

Aria took off, and I stood in front of Nine's in deep thought. It took me more than a minute to switch gears. I was used to being the one to swoop in and take charge, to take care of my bestie, but Aria didn't need me to now because she was marrying an amazing man. Vince texted me less than ten minutes later to say that he'd have everything taken care of and to stand by for an updated itinerary.

I had to do a mental check to see how I felt about all this. Guys had come and gone out of our lives, but I had always taken care of Aria. Even her late husband, Raja, was content with letting me be in charge. If felt weird to not have to do that now.

I exhaled and wondered if chocolate would address my feelings, but the answer was no. I stepped off the sidewalk and headed toward my truck, driving to the only other place I knew to go.

No, it wasn't to Finn's. Although, I wished he was home for the umpteenth time that week.

My mom was in the kitchen in her floral nightgown, getting ready to put her evening tea on—a ritual I had seen her do a thousand times. Through the front window, I watched her fill the kettle with her filtered water, place her tea leaves in her infuser, and then select her favorite cup to enjoy it all in when it was done. She must've seen me out front because she didn't even flinch when I opened the back door.

"Would you like a cup?" she asked.

"Sure, why not." I peered into the living room and saw my dad dozing in his recliner, a baseball game on the TV. Both men in my life had a love for the MLB. Another reason why my dad probably liked Finn so much.

I took a seat at the oak kitchen table and waited for my mom to join me. She brought over two mugs of tea and a little plate of cookies, and sat.

"Thanks, Mom. This is nice." I stirred some honey into my cup and took a sip. It wasn't chai, but the chamomile would probably do a better job of calming me.

My mom doctored up her tea and took a couple sips, letting the silence linger for a moment longer until she felt compelled to break it. She may be prim and proper, but she also knew when to pry.

"I know Finn's out of town, so this can't be about him," she finally said. She was right. I had done a lot of thinking about Finn over the course of the week, probably too much. I knew where I stood with him. Now I just needed to fill *him* in.

No, everything felt right in the relationship department.

It wasn't really Aria's impending wedding that had me feeling all philosophical either. Although, that may have started me down the path of self-reflection. No, this was about Justine and Todd and the way it made me feel, like I had been sucker punched. Christina might have tampered with my products, but I had no way of knowing if she had also cancelled with the realtor or stolen my product shipment, and I doubted she'd be confessing to it anytime soon. Justine and Todd could very well still be behind it. The fact that two people could potentially hate me enough to team up and plan my demise didn't sit well with me or my karma.

"Do you think I'm a good person?" I asked my mom.

"Well, I'm pretty fond of you. I think your father, and Finn, and Aria would all think so."

"I don't think you guys count."

"Whose opinion are you worried about?"

"Justine's?"

My mom raised her eyebrows. I hadn't given a hoot about what Justine thought for a long time.

"It's just, someone's been going through a lot of trouble to mess with my life right now and I think it might be her, again."

"Well, maybe it's time you mended that fence."

"What, you mean like say sorry and make up? Mom, this isn't grade school."

"I know, but you two have been feuding for years, and it hasn't done you any good. Maybe you should try a different approach."

I stared at my mom for a long minute. She didn't blink. I did not want to be friends with Justine. But I was also sick of dealing with her crap year after year. It had to stop.

"You know, they say that forgiveness isn't something that we do for other people, it's something that we do for ourselves," my mother added.

I rolled my eyes. "You really gotta stop watching the Hallmark Channel.

"Just think about it."

I wrinkled my nose and took another sip of tea. Sometimes I hated it when my mother was right.

21

*S*omeone woke me up at eight AM by banging on my front door. Captain Jack growled something fierce and I was about to join in. Anyone who knew me was aware that you didn't wake me up before nine, and you sure as heck didn't stop by before ten, unless it was an emergency.

The person knocked again. *Whoever this is better hope it's an emergency.* I literally rolled out of bed. Captain Jack decided to stay. I gave him the evil eye as I shuffled toward the front door. I looked out my peep hole and saw a guy in full bicycle gear with an envelope in his hand. I looked down to see if what I was wearing was appropriate enough to answer the door in. I had slept in a pair of black yoga pants and an off-the-shoulder lightweight sweatshirt. A favorite of mine. I couldn't have been the only person who turned up the air conditioning at night just so I could wear warm, comfy clothes, right?

The messenger went to knock again and I swung the door open. I may have even snarled. The guy winced. "Sorry, my directions specifically said to keep knocking."

I didn't say a word, just held out my hand for the enve-lope. My name was handwritten in script across the front and the back had a wax seal with an old English *D* stamped into it. *Ah, Aria's wedding itinerary. Of course.* Only Vince would send someone out to hand-deliver wedding invita-tions at sunrise. How Aria's fiancé had managed such an elaborate invitation on such short notice was beyond me. He operated on an entirely different level of wealth that us commoners couldn't even comprehend. However, when I opened the envelope, I saw that the stationary only contained a list, a packing list to be exact, with a request to bring my passport, along with the time that my driver would be picking me up tomorrow afternoon. Aria was officially marrying an international man of mystery.

I walked back to my bedroom and looked inside the door. Captain Jack had moved over to my spot and was being a total bed hog. I think he was smiling in his sleep. I thought about moving him, but truthfully, I probably wasn't going to be able to fall back asleep. *No point in disrupting the cutie patootie.*

I walked into the living room instead, grabbed the throw off the back of the couch, and cuddled up with my phone. I was doing my usual morning routine—checking email and scrolling through my newsfeed, when I saw a late-breaking news article: "Candidate Exposed." The lead photo was a picture of Whip running naked around Mrs. DeVine's back-yard. I was certain it was one of the photos that goofy guy had taken. Whip's private parts had been blurred out, but his face was clearly in focus. The article read:

Mayoral candidate Whip McGovern has been charged with indecent exposure after streaking naked through the upscale neighborhood of Sweetwater last night. The candidate's campaign manager, Ms. Holly Fitz, stated that the candidate had been recently prescribed a muscle relaxer for a recurring lacrosse injury and believed Mr. Whip suffered from an adverse side effect.

Yeah, shrinkage, I thought.

Mr. McGovern would like to take this opportunity to remind people how dangerous prescription medication can be, and to read all possible side effects. If you ever have any concerns, you should discuss them with your doctor.

Well, there was a shocker. Whip chose not to take any accountability. Heaven forbid he apologize for his actions. I sincerely hoped he was done being interested in me. I closed the article and brought up the notepad app on my phone, making a list of everything I needed to do. With Aria's wedding in her groom's hands, I could finally focus on getting my business back on track. However, I couldn't do that until I had some caffeine in my system. I managed to shower up, get dressed, do my hair and makeup, and Captain Jack was still snoozing. This time, I woke the pup so he could go outside and do his business before I left for Sweet Thangs. Captain Jack wasn't happy, but he came around to the idea after he heard the kibble hit his bowl. With his needs taken care of, I locked up and headed out for my beloved chai latte.

THURSDAY MORNINGS TENDED to see an uptake in visitors to our small coastal town. It was still nothing like last weekend's Seaside Days, but Sweet Thangs did have a bit of a line. I was perfectly content to play on my phone and wait my turn, until I spotted Justine and Todd, holding hands in line a few spots ahead of me.

I gave an inward sigh. This had to be the universe's way of testing out my mother's theory. I exhaled and decided I would try and be nice. However, I wasn't making any promises. The two were still waiting for their order to come up after I had placed mine. I know Justine spotted me when she started hanging on Todd and getting all touchy-feely with him. Once again, I couldn't have cared less. I knew what he looked like under those clothes. It wasn't anything to brag about. Not like Finn.

Todd's posture stiffened when I approached them. Justine practically wrapped her legs around him as if to say, *"He's mine!"* I snickered.

"Hey, guys, I didn't know you two were dating. That's great." I tried to give a genuine smile. My eye twitched from the effort. Justine seemed to be waiting for the insult, but I left it at that. Believe me, it was hard. I would've loved to throw in something about Todd needing to watch out that her hair didn't bleach his sheets, or maybe giving him a friendly reminder that the county health department offered free STD screenings, but I didn't.

"Yeah, well..." Justine started a retort, but it made absolutely no sense, seeing that she hadn't been insulted.

"What was that?" I asked as if she had been trying to say something nice. They both just stared at me. I heard the barista call Justine's name. "Oh, sounds like your drinks are up. I'll let you get to it. Nice seeing you." I waved them off and stood back, still waiting on my drink.

They continued to stare at me.

"Your drinks. Right there," I said, pointing. "They're ready." The barista then said my name. "And it looks like mine is too." I walked past them, grabbed my drink, dropped a dollar in the tip cup, and walked out. I didn't dare look back over my shoulder.

I stepped outside into the bright sunshine and smiled.

That had been oddly satisfying. Maybe my mom was onto something after all.

A second later, my cell phone rang. It was Cassandra. I literally squeezed my eyes shut when I answered the phone, hoping for good news. If not, I might have to go back inside Sweet Thangs and do a one-eighty on Justine and Todd.

"Hey, Ziva, it's Cassandra. Listen, I've got some great news. That space is available if you still want it."

"Yes, absolutely! When can we sign?" I was not risking losing that storefront again.

Cassandra said we could do it now, which was perfect timing for me. I headed over to her office to get the paperwork done. For as much stress securing the place had caused me, it was relatively easy to make it mine. A handful of signatures and a small fortune later, I had the keys in my hand. I couldn't wait to tell Finn. It was going to be awesome. I had a shop—Sugar & Sass Skincare—and it was all mine.

Now that I had a storefront ready to go, I really needed to focus on my products and marketing. I had to get that new logo finalized and think about signage, business cards, labels, anything and everything that would sport my business name. While I thought about that, I got to work mixing up a new idea I had been kicking around for a honey-sugar facial scrub. The recipe was simple. I simply mixed equal parts honey, brown sugar, and olive oil. I was finally going to get a chance to work with Suzanne's honey, (which was delicious, by the way), and the best part was, I was going to test the product out on myself. I could've really used some pampering right about then.

I mixed the ingredients and, once set, I pulled my hair back from my face and tested it out by splashing some lukewarm water on my face and applying the scrub. It felt wonderful, or it would, I had no doubt, once I washed it off. I had been right to go with the brown sugar versus white in the mix. Brown sugar provided just the right level of coarseness, sloughing off the dead skin without being too harsh. Captain Jack cocked his head and looked at me like I had lost my mind, while I cleaned up the kitchen and let the mask soak in. I offered to put some on him, but he turned tail and ran for the bedroom.

I left the mask on for about five minutes and then washed it off. It was perfect. My skin glowed. It was baby smooth. I had no doubt that my customers would love it.

And then my face started to feel all tingly.

I started feeling all tingly.

And goofy, like I had slammed one too many tequila shots and I either needed to hit the dance floor or take a nap.

I chose to take a nap, or rather, the nap chose me. I lay down right then and there on my living room floor, barely able to grab a throw pillow off the couch before it was lights-out.

I had no idea what time it was when I woke. It was still light out, but the sun appeared to be setting. My head pounded and my mouth was dry; it was like a wicked hangover on steroids. Captain Jack was curled up around my legs and tried to lick my face as soon as he realized I had awoken.

I sat up slowly. "It's okay, buddy. I'm okay," I tried to reassure my pup. *What the heck was that?* I was clueless. *Was my sugar too low?* No, it shouldn't have been. I had stopped and picked up a meatball sub after signing the lease papers, so my stomach had been full, and for once it wasn't just with sugar.

Then I thought back to last night and everyone else who

had been acting goofy, as if they were drunk. I giggled, remembering Whip's naked butt.

"Sweet sugar, that's it!" Leave it to a naked butt to have it all make sense.

I got up off the floor a little too quickly and my vision swam for a second. "I'm okay," I told Captain Jack. He looked skeptical. "See?" I did a little jig. "It's all good. Now, let's take you out for a second so I can get out of here."

I'd figured out what had happened, at least last night and this afternoon, but possibly with the whole case. I was also almost convinced it was one big accident. I just needed one other piece of the puzzle before I'd know for sure.

inding Suzanne Butterfield's farm at night proved to be trickier than I expected. More than once, I thought I must've have driven past it, but finally I saw the white farmhouse up ahead. The driveway was marked with an address reflector, making it easier to spot the entrance, and ensured that I didn't tear up her yard. I wasn't sure if she'd be home, or there was a chance that Jeffery was home and not up for visitors. However, this was too big for me to sit on. I got out of my truck and looked around. The house was dark from where I stood, and the front light was off, but I could see light glowing from the back of the house.

I walked around the side of the house and was surprised to find Suzanne outside, tending to her bees. I remembered her saying something about how they usually moved the hives at night and thought maybe that's what she was up to, until I realized that she was pacing back and forth. Suzanne walked up and down the rows, muttering to herself. The closer I got, the more I could tell that she was out of it. She didn't even see me approach when I heard her say, "Can't tell Jeffery. Can't tell Humphrey. What to do? What to do?"

I was initially thinking that she had figured it out. I was right. It was an accident. I was about to interrupt her and tell her it would be okay when she said, "Have to kill her. No other choice. I see it now."

Say what? Kill who? Suzanne was probably less than twenty feet in front of me. I dropped to the ground and crawled behind one of the hive boxes. I could hear the humming of the bees inside and it gave me the creepy crawlies. *Worst hiding spot ever, Ziva.* I waited a second to see how this would play out. I peered around the hive box and saw Suzanne walking in the darkness across her yard toward a tool shed. She disappeared inside and I started to follow to get a closer look, only to dive bomb behind another bee box when she popped back out with a shovel in her hand.

Oh, sweet sugar! Who is she going to whack with that? But she didn't whack anyone. She walked over to another smaller outbuilding on the property and jammed the shovel through the building's handle, forcefully locking it.

"An unfortunate accident. That's what we have here. Nothing more. Get it done and taken care of. Move on," she said. Nothing like a little homicide pep talk to get you going.

I had obviously greatly underestimated Suzanne. I thought Whip was a power-hungry sociopath. Suzanne took that title to a whole other level.

The crazy woman walked toward the barn on the far side of the property and I thought this was my chance to free whomever she had locked up inside. I made a run for it across the yard and over to the building. The building, about the size of a small garage, had two square windows on the side. Standing on my tiptoes, I peered in and found Vicki, bound and gagged, tied to a chair. The way her head was slumped forward told me she was unconscious and, hopefully, not yet dead.

I looked around to find something to help me get into the building. I didn't dare try and move the shovel jammed in the door as I was afraid Suzanne would see me. It was safer staying on the side.

A small woodpile had been stacked up along the back of the building. I ran over and grabbed two pieces, using them to give me a boost. It was just enough to raise the window. It was not easy to pull myself in. *Must. Go. To. The. Gym.* The whole not-working-out thing really wasn't working out. My arms shook just from pulling myself up and over. I hit the floor harder than I had expected; especially seeing that I hit a workbench on my way in.

I stayed crouched down for a minute, rubbing my backside and giving my eyes a chance to adjust to the darkness. I was right in that the building was nothing more than a garage used to store lawn equipment. In the middle of it was a rather large riding lawnmower. I already decided I was going to ride that baby out of there if I got the chance. *Suzanne had better get ready to run.*

I moved in the dark over to Vicki and began to untie the bandana that she had been gagged with. She snapped her head up and darted it side to side, ready to fight. Her glasses had been knocked off her face, and were a couple feet beside her. Even in the dark, I could tell her face was puffy from the blow.

I came around to the front of her. "Vicki, it's me, Ziva," I wasn't sure how well she could see me. I could see her though. Her eyes were full of fear. I put her glasses back on her face. "Hold still and let me get this off you." I went back behind her and worked on getting the gag loose. I couldn't get it completely untied, but managed to get it loose enough to fall around her neck.

In a hoarse voice, almost a whisper, Vicki warned, "It's the honey." I immediately began working on the rope that bound her to the chair. I wasn't sure when Suzanne would come back, but I didn't want to be sitting there when she did.

"I know. I figured that out this afternoon. What's wrong with it?" I knew it had made me sick, but I didn't understand how.

"It's called mad honey. It happens when bees pollinate toxic rhododendron flowers and make honey from their nectar." Vicki coughed and cleared her throat.

"Do people do that on purpose?"

"Absolutely. All you need to do is move a hive next to the flowers."

I remembered Suzanne telling me she moved hives, and I told Vicki so.

"That's all she had to do. The bees took care of the rest. People have been using the honey as a weapon for centuries. Even leading to the fall of the Roman army in 67 B.C." Leave it to Vicki to give me a horticulture lesson while being held hostage in a storage shed.

"I thought it was an accident though?"

"So did I. Big mistake. Guess she had to climb that social ladder one way or another," Vicki said, looking down at her bound feet. "I just hope Jeffery's okay. She said something about this being all his fault."

"I doubt that."

I was just getting Vicki's hands free when the other garage window slid open. We both froze. Suzanne was in the window, chucking in chunks of honeycomb and dumping an entire bee hive through the window. She didn't see us. She was too bent on carrying out her master plan. The garage immediately filled with angry, buzzing bees. Vicki's feet were still tied to the chair, but even if she could've run, I wasn't sure where we were going to go. The bees were heaviest by the window, plus I had no idea where Suzanne was. For all I knew, she was standing outside the garage with a shotgun. At this point, I wouldn't put anything past her. A riding lawnmower wasn't going to cut it.

I crouched back down on the ground and focused on freeing Vicki. After that, we could plan our escape.

Just then, I felt the sharp bite on the back of my neck and another one on the back of my arm in rapid succession. I brushed at the back of my arm to shoo the bee and pain away, and grabbed my arm. It hurt like crazy and I wanted to scream. It was the most intense itching and burning sensation I had ever felt. My arm and neck immediately started to swell and a burning sensation spread throughout my body.

Vicki managed to take off her shoes and free herself before I had been able to untie the ropes around her feet. Everything felt like it was moving in slow motion. My hands trembled and my throat felt scratchy, and it hurt to swallow, like something was stick in there. The burning sensation then made its way to my stomach, such a hot pain. I would've given anything to jump in a cold bath and let the frigid water take the heat away. I swore if I survived this bee attack, I was never going to eat honey again.

Vicki knew something was wrong right away. Probably because I was practically having a panic attack on the garage floor. I was trying not to let the fear take over, but when you can't breathe and are in intense pain, it's kind of hard not to.

"Bees," I managed to wheeze out.

"You're allergic?" she asked.

I nodded. Vicki helped me up and hid me under the

work bench while she searched the garage. The way she moved about in the dark told me she had been in here before. I was huddled under the work bench, focusing on breathing in and out, when Vicki came back over in front of me, carrying a large case. Putting the case down, she undid the clips and flipped it open. It was a chainsaw. With a couple of tweaks and few pulls, the beast roared to life. I didn't even ask her what she was doing. She walked right over to the wooden garage doors and cut right into them. If Suzanne was anywhere close, she'd better start running. The chainsaw ate up those doors like they were nothing. Vicki hauled off and gave the doors a solid kick and they fell forward, crashing to the ground. A man yelled in surprise. It was Jeffery. He stood in the opening, a parade of police cars and firetrucks lighting up the sky behind him. Vicki dropped the chainsaw and Jeffrey ran to her, embracing her in the biggest display of lip-locked PDA anyone had ever witnessed. *Ah, so that's why Vicki stuck around the mean girls; she has the hots for Suzanne's stepson.* I would've thought it to be an epic scene, had I not been on the verge of passing out.

THE BACK of the ambulance doors had been left open as I sat there with an EMT by my side. I was beyond thankful that the cavalry had also included an ambulance. Within a couple of minutes, I was feeling much better thanks to Benadryl and epinephrine. The medicine was administered in time to stop my allergic reaction. I was a bit twitchy, but at least I could breathe. Forget lipstick, Benadryl and an Epi-Pen were going to be my new must-have accessories. The medic was ready to take me to the hospital, but I was still trying to talk my way out of that one.

Vicki sat next to me with an ice pack on her face, while another medic tended to her bee stings. She had been stung a handful of times, but luckily hadn't had any adverse reaction besides the typical pain. A couple more ice packs and ibuprofen was all she needed. Jeffery stood outside the ambulance waiting, rather impatiently. I had a feeling he wouldn't be leaving her side anytime soon.

I thanked Jeffery for all his help. "How did you know?" I asked, meaning where Vicki and I were.

"A bit of luck, really. I had finally decided that the business wasn't worth it. I was upstairs packing a few things when I heard Vicki scream. I looked out the window and saw Suzanne drag her into the shed." Yep, I was thinking a whole lot of luck and maybe a little bit of my nan. *Thank you*, I said to my guardian angel.

"Knowing how crazy Suzanne is, I immediately called nine-one-one before trying to be a hero," Jeffery added.

"Smart." Maybe I should try that sometime? I looked down at my swollen arm. It was a total puffy mess.

I glanced over to see that Mayor Potts had arrived on the scene. He was practically jumping in front of Detective Roxy, trying to get a word in, while she handcuffed Suzanne. Apparently, the mad woman hadn't made it very far. "Please listen. Listen! I don't understand. This doesn't make any sense. Suzanne, tell them you didn't do this!" he pleaded with them. The mayor obviously hadn't been in on it. You couldn't fake that level of desperation. He looked to be another one of Suzanne's victims. Ah, the power of a woman. I'm betting he was so enthralled with her wanting him that he turned a blind eye to her wrongdoings. I had a feeling their relationship was a recent affair for him to be that enamored.

Suzanne, however, was ignoring Humphrey, instead

shouting for Jeffery like usual. "JEFFERY! Where is he? This is all his fault!" She even stomped her foot. "I'm not going anywhere! Find that fool!"

"She murders someone and it's my fault. Ridiculous," Jeffery said to us. Suzanne still had no idea where he was and continued to yell and curse his name.

"What does she mean?" I asked Jeffery.

"She made toxic honey, right? And then, instead of getting rid of it, stored it with our specialty blends. So, next to the gallberry and clover honeys, she puts something that can kill a person."

"That was dumb," I said. *And she thought Jeffery was the thick one.*

"Exactly, so of course I don't know that, and end up packaging it as gallberry. It looks the same. I even put it on our own kitchen table."

"Which, I'm guessing is how the mayor got poisoned?"

"Most likely."

"Did you know they were a thing?"

"Oh yeah."

"Why do you think she did it?"

"To get rid of Paulette. She knew Humphrey was cheating on her, but she still wouldn't leave him; their relationship was more for show, so you know Humphrey wasn't about to break up with her either. Guess Suzanne got tired of playing second fiddle."

I looked over at Mayor Potts. *All this, over him? Really?* Baby blue suits and polka dot bow ties just didn't do it for me. Not to mention, he lacked common sense. Why anyone would murder a friend over a man was beyond me.

"So yeah, none of this is my fault. I'm just thankful that none of the bottles I packaged killed anyone," Jeffery added. *Nope, just knocked me on my butt for a couple hours.*

I had to do a bit of a double take when the goofy guy with the fedora and trench coat showed up on the scene. He was videoing Suzanne being arrested. The bright light from his phone shone right in her eyes.

"You put that phone down right this second, Kevin. Do you hear me? I do NOT want you filming this!" Kevin wasn't listening. "Kevin! You and your brother, I swear!"

I looked at Jeffery. "Your brother?"

Jeffery shook his head like he couldn't believe it. "Suzanne hired him to dig up dirt on Whip, but I think he took it too far. He's a little different." Kevin filmed the entire scene until Detective Roxy put an end to the matter and took away his phone. I thought I heard Kevin say something like "shucks" and that he was going to get his backup camera.

I lay my head back and closed my eyes. I couldn't wait to tell all this to Finn. Was it Saturday yet?

23

I drove down to the courthouse to pick up Mrs. J. With the case now solved, she was free to go. Last night had been eventful in more ways than one. It was the middle of the night by the time I got home from the hospital. Thankfully, I hadn't had a secondary reaction and was released after a short observation. With a filled Epi-pen prescription and a couple bottles of Benadryl, I was ready for Aria's wedding, wherever it was going to be. I still had three hours until my driver was scheduled to pick me up, plenty of time to grab Mrs. J. and get home to finish packing.

The front of the courthouse was packed with reporters and television crews huddled around a podium. Detective Roxy was in the middle of them. She sported a pair of jeans with a brown suede jacket over a white shirt. Her makeup looked completely natural. If she was a knock out before, then she was drop dead gorgeous now. I'd like to think that it had been courtesy of my beauty catalogs.

"Is this about Suzanne?" I asked when I got out. Kevin had gone public with all the extra footage he had, documenting Suzanne and Humphrey's affair. The scandal was all over the news. I figured with Paulette's murder being such a high-profile case now, it warranted a news conference.

I was wrong.

"Ha, not hardly," Detective Roxy said.

"What's going on then?"

"You're going to have to ask Mrs. J. when she comes out."

"She called this event?" *Oh boy. This ought to be good.* I wasn't sure if I should go inside and get her, and figure out what this was all about, or just wait for her to come out. After five minutes, I decided to fetch her when she made her entrance. Mrs. J. walked out of the court house dressed head to toe in peach. Satin peach hat, peach chiffon dress, and peach heels. The only thing on her that wasn't peach were her pearls.

"New jail house digs?" I joked with Roxy.

"Heck no. One of her lady friends came by and helped her get ready. She was released two hours ago."

Mrs. J. approached the podium and eyed the microphones, apparently pleased by the number of attendees. "You guys filming?" she asked, pointing to the cameramen. They nodded that they were. "Good, good." She then cleared her throat and proceeded to say, "I just wanted to thank y'all for coming down here today. This is a big day, especially after my recent hardships." Mrs. J. looked at the courthouse behind her. She had spent less than two full days in jail, but she wasn't going to let anyone forget that anytime soon. "Being falsely imprisoned has taught me something: you have to fight for what you love. And I love this town," she said, hammering on the podium. A couple of older ladies in the background clapped on cue. "Port Haven has seen a lot of change. A lot of change, folks, and it hasn't been good. No, it hasn't. It's a darn disgrace the scandal our current mayor's in, not to mention the joke of a candidate running against him. Did y'all see him without his drawers? We can't have that. Port Haven deserves better. I've decided that there needs to be new management in this town, which is why I would like to take this opportunity to formally announce my candidacy for mayor!" Mrs. J. gave a winning smile. Detective Roxy and I couldn't help but clap. I think everyone else was speechless. I had no doubt Mrs. J. would make one heck of a mayor. With the dirt she had on people, I was sure she'd be able to get things done. She had my vote. Now she just needed to get in the car. I had a wedding to get ready for.

I WAS FINALLY THERE, in my paradise. One would've thought the wedding would've taken place on Vince's private Caribbean island, but that wasn't original enough. No, we were in the southern heart of the Pacific Ocean on a small island off the coast of New Caledonia. Aria and Vince had chosen a sunrise wedding (I know, don't get me started!) I may have been half asleep, but even I could see that Aria looked stunning in her gown. The rose gold dress, coupled with the pinks and oranges in the sunrise, made for a beyond-beautiful portrait. Vince had completed the brunch reception with plenty of champagne, exotic fresh fruits, savory crepes, and my favorite—chocolate-filled croissants. The morning had been a whirlwind, but by eleven AM, the festivities were complete and I was officially off maid-of-honor duty.

Shades on, toes in the sand, drink by my side ... this was the life. Finally, I was ready to relax. They were going to have to pry me from those white sand beaches when it was time to go. I seriously would've loved to extend my vacation, if only I could've afforded it. Who knew, maybe my business would take off and I could relocate to someplace more tropical like this. Heck, maybe Finn would even be down for it. Just looking at the water I thought the fishing had to be phenomenal. Hello, it was the South Pacific. I'm sure he would jump at a chance to run a fishing charter down here. I smiled. *Look at me, planning a future with a man.* Okay, so it was all in my head right now, but it was a start.

"What are you smiling about?" said a familiar voice that made my heart do a little flip flop. I opened my eyes to see my beau standing above me. Bare chested, board shorts on, a can of Coke in his hand. Mmm, he was a sight.

"Finn!" I jumped up and into his arms, wrapping my legs around his waist and almost knocking him over. I kissed him as if he had been out to sea for a year, not a week. His can of Coke lay forgotten in the sand.

"And I thought you didn't like surprises," he said, a little breathless. I jumped down. "Not that I'm complaining. We can do that again."

I kissed him again.

"That just made that ridiculously long flight worth it," he said.

"If you thought that made it worth it, just wait until later," I teased.

"Long week?"

"Very,' I replied. Finn had no idea. It was going to take more than a minute to get him caught up to speed, but truthfully, that wasn't a priority. I had something else I wanted to discuss with him.

"So, I did a lot of thinking this week, and here's the thing. I really missed you. Like hardcore. More than I thought I would," I sai.

"Good, because I missed you too." Finn took my hand.

"You did?"

"I didn't just fly around the world for some girl. I did it for *my* girl."

"Aww, I'm your girl?"

"For as long you want to be," he said.

"I like that." Because right then, I wanted to be his girl for a very long time.

EYELINER & ALIBIS

BEAUTY SECRETS SERIES BOOK 3

Dear Reader,

Ziva solved the last case like the girl boss she is, but is she up to the challenge again?

Ziva's television debut is a complete disaster, and when the host at fault is murdered, the detective sets her eyes on Ziva. As Ziva races to clear her name, the killer gets ready to strike again.

It's another case full of the twists and turns you've come to expect from Beauty Secrets. So grab some chocolate and a chai latte and start sleuthing again with Eyeliner & Alibis.

A RING TO DIE FOR

FREE BEAUTY SECRETS SHORT STORY

There's no gold at the end of this rainbow...

Ziva's best friend has been framed for robbing a jewelry store and it's up to Ziva to crack the case. The situation quickly turns deadly and suddenly a robbery is fool's gold compared to what Ziva uncovers. The search for the killer leads Ziva straight into his crosshairs. Will she be able to take him down before he makes his mark?

Download it HERE

ABOUT THE AUTHOR

I'm a mystery author with a soft spot for romance and humor, too. I love all things girlie with a dollop of danger, have a strong affinity for the color pink (especially in diamonds and champagne), and, not to brag, but chocolate and I are in a pretty serious relationship. My books feature fearless females, a little bit of love, a few laughs, and a whole lot of whodunit. I hope my stories keep you guessing and laughing all the way until the end.

www.stephaniedamore.com
steph.damore@gmail.com

 facebook.com/stephdamoreauthor

twitter.com/stephdamore

 instagram.com/steph_damore_author

14754201R00118

Printed in Great Britain
by Amazon